AMERICAN DISEASE

Jay Bajaj

Smart House Books
TORONTO, ONTARIO

Heidi von Palleske/Smart House Books
100 Bain Ave., Toronto, On., M4K1E8

Publisher's Note: This is a work of fiction. Names, characters, places, and incidents are a product of the author's imagination. Locales and public names are sometimes used for atmospheric purposes. Any resemblance to actual people, living or dead, or to businesses, companies, events, institutions, or locales is completely coincidental.

Front cover image by Steven Miric
Author image by Prithi Yelaja
Cover design by Aaron Rachel Brown

ISBN 978-1-988980-10-2

To
My family
Who are going think all this fiction is fact
And hate me, regardless.
Jay

AMERICAN DISEASE

His Number One sister had updated him on all the family gossip in the three days since his arrival in India. Now, climbing the stairs to the third-floor government flat of his Number Two sister, his Number One sister's earlier warning flashed in his mind:

"As she is getting older, she's becoming very cantankerous. She won't take any medication, refuses to listen to anybody. She has given up cooking, cleaning and everything else. And you know all about that lazy, pompous husband of hers. He is useless. Poor Monica, has to do all the housework herself before she goes to the office. Neither one of them care anything about her. Now Monica is almost 25 and they still haven't found her a suitable boy to marry. Terrible! Their only daughter!"

Jag's Number Two sister was married to a senior central-government official in New Delhi. He ran his home in the same bureaucratic fashion as his office, treating his wife and daughter like lowly clerks and peons. In the last few years, however, his oldest sister had become hilariously blunt. She simply told the truth as she saw it, without any embarrassment.

From the hallway on the third floor Jag could see the twenty-year-old wooden name-plate of his brother-in-law still hanging on the door. The letters were painted in yellow italic letters over an old varnished wood coloured plate, with his educational qualification and his job position in the government tacked onto the end of his name. The name plate was still considered a status symbol from the old British days. Some high officials chose to continue with the plaques to make themselves look more British-like. It was as though the name-plate implied that the person living inside was, somehow, more sophisticated.

Jag rang the bell and waited. The ring was not a soft chime like in Canada, but loud and jarring, like an old alarm clock.

Looking at the name-plate again, Jag wondered how much India had changed after its independence. The old pompousness and greed of the British in the earlier days had been taken over by bureaucrats and politicians. Mahatma Gandhi's high morals had been conveniently forgotten so that money could be the real power. Although the painted plaque remained as a reminder of better times, Jag knew that his Number Two brother-in-law had become a pretentious high moral bureaucrat and, therefore, a moneyless dud.

After a few minutes of waiting, Jag rang the bell again and noticed that the lens from the peephole was missing. He pressed his eye to the hole. It was dark inside.

Number One sister had warned that he would probably have to ring three or four times and wait several minutes before Number Two sister would answer the door. "It takes her a long time to get up these days."

2

He waited and took in his surroundings. The yellow plaster, typical of all government quarters in New Delhi, was peeling. The cement floor had several cracks. It was a building reserved for the first-class gazetted officers of the central government. Idly looking, Jag mused about how lower-class quarters would compare. Like all systems in India, this building seemed to be in disrepair; another victim of neglect and corruption.

He rang the bell one last time, holding his finger firmly on the button, letting it ring for a solid minute.

"Who?" The abrupt, loud bark of his Number Two sister came through. She always spoke in minimal words. For her, speaking in complete sentences was a waste of time. She did all her work quickly and efficiently with her quick, loud mouth.

"Me," Jag shouted back through the peephole, purposely not saying his name to see if she still recognized his voice.

"Who?" she repeated. Jag realized that she was probably still in bed and didn't feel inclined to get up to answer the door.

"It's Jag!" He hurriedly blurted out his name.

His sister's voice sounded excited. "Ah! wait!"

Jag could hear her chappal's click-clack approaching the door. Then he saw an eye in the empty peephole and, finally, his Number Two sister opened the door. She gave him a big bear-hug and then started to complain in her short sentences, "In India ... three days... now you find time to visit... Ha? Come... come." She did not believe in small smiles so just laughed out loud through her missing teeth.

The door opened into the living room. There had not been any changes since Jag had last visited her five years ago. The room was dusty and dark, neglected. Jag looked at his sister. Even she looked old and disheveled. She had been such a beautiful and outgoing girl in her younger days, but there was no trace of that old fire in her face now. Sadness started to creep up on Jag, wrapping around him like an old woolen sweater.

They had lost everything in the partition of India, becoming refugees in their own country. Before that, before his mother had to sell the last of her dowry to pay for his sister's dowry, there had been better days. Jag remembered the engagement, arranged by their grandfather for his Number Two sister because he was so proud of that particular grand-daughter. Not only was she very pretty, but she could read a few words of English! At that time, any girl who could read a few words of English was considered 'highly educated.' And then, after their grandfather died, they became displaced people in India and their father was unable to marry her off because he could not afford the demands of a large cash dowry her would-be in-laws were insisting upon. Number One sister had been married off when she was just fifteen, and Number Two was still not married at twenty! This was a very big burden and a shame for Jag's family. Jag remembered it well, although he was only five at the time. He remembered the sadness in his mother's eyes when she finally decided to sell off the last of her jewelry to pay that dowry.

"Come, come. Sit," she said loudly, breaking through Jag's distracted thoughts. But before he could even dust the chair with his handkerchief she began her interrogation of him.

"Heard you quit your job. Sick or what? What do you do all day if you aren't working?"

She examined him from top to bottom, searching for signs of disease. Jag shook his head. He was not prepared for such a quick cross-examination. He knew it would be very hard to explain to her why he would quit a perfectly good job in Canada just to take a year off to travel.

"No... not sick – just a mid-life crisis perhaps," he tried to explain weakly.

"Is that an American disease?"

"I live in Canada," he protested. "And no, it's not a disease. I'm just trying to sort out my values, my life."

She was not going be satisfied by any evasiveness. "Then what is this quitting your job, growing long hair and a ponytail like a girl? Have you come back to India to become a sadhu, or a ganja-smoking hippie?" She barked a laugh at her own joke.

Jag shrugged his shoulders and let her be happy with her laughter. When her laughter settled, he changed the subject, hinting that he had been well-briefed on family affairs.

"Have you found a suitable boy for Monica yet, or are you planning to keep her unmarried and save the dowry?" He asked his Number Two sister.

Despite her bluntness and ability to laugh at anybody and anything at any moment, this matter was a sore point for his sister. Having an unmarried, twenty-five-year-old daughter was a family shame for any middle-class mother, especially when the father happened to be a pompous class-one-gazetted officer in the central government.

She focussed on Jag. "Now that you're here for a few days, you can help me find a suitable boy for your favourite niece!"

In India, people often transfer the burdens of personal guilt and family shame by simply changing a few words like 'my only daughter' to 'your favourite niece.' Jag had been away long enough to have forgotten those tricks but, in order to feel useful again, to overcome his vague depression of his so-called American mid- life crisis, he was quick to accept his sister's request for help. Of course, his Number Two sister also knew that, because he was the most generous of the siblings, Jag would happily spend his North American money to travel around in taxis, making it much more comfortable for her and her miserly husband to go along with them.

"Ah, good. Bring your things here and stay with us a few days. Monica will be very happy."

Poor Monica, as Jag had been warned, was burdened with all the chores of the housework and now she had the added burden of caring for Jag's needs such as boiled water and non-spicy cooking. His sister having given up on everyday work, and life in general, just expected Monica to do the extra work. Jag's brother-in-law felt it was his privilege not to do anything at all as he was the man and the head of the house. Jag said nothing about the inequities of this household. He decided to tolerate the outdated beliefs if only to help his niece get free of her duties. Yes, he would find her a suitable boy as soon as possible.

The following morning, after Monica and Jag's grandiose brother-in-law left for their offices, Jag's Number Two sister finally got out of bed. She brought her bed-tea to the balcony, along with The Hindustan Times. As she passed the newspaper to Jag she asked, "Did you check the matrimonial column in today's paper?"

"Nothing special," he nodded.

She sat down on the cot under the sun and opened the newspaper to check the matrimonial ads herself. In the December warm sunlight, she arranged her one-armed reading glasses and started to examine the ad section carefully.

Jag watched her finger moving slowly through each line while she read loudly, "Needed for a handsome boy, twenty-five, five feet tall from a pure Hindu family with very good business, a homely, educated, pretty fair-skinned girl, who is also good in cooking. Apply with photo. Dowry negotiable."

'Homely' in India means a girl with traditional family values. Jag couldn't help smiling as he thought how different the word was in North America. He imagined an election campaign, promising a return to 'homely values!'

As his Number Two sister read, she pushed her glasses back up her nose at the end of each ad, only to have them slip back down as she started the next sentence.

"Don't you think these arranged marriages and dowry demand systems are out of place in the 20th century?" He asked.

Her reply was immediate and scathing. "And what country did you say you live in?" She openly smiled, her yellowish, gap-filled teeth in full display.

"But what about Monica? She is educated, modern and westernized. She has a very good job and makes good money. She may not like this arranged marriage idea," he tried to argue.

Number Two sister felt it unnecessary to respond to any such blasphemous heresy from her Canadianized little brother. She gave him a *what's-wrong-with-you-boy* glare and went back to her matrimonial ads, but this time she stopped reading them aloud.

Finally she broke the silence between them and spoke in a concerned tone, "We've registered Monica with the local 'Panchayat.' The Pundit took her horoscope and the fee last week, but has not come back with any prospects. Why don't you go and check with him?"

Jag agreed to go that afternoon. Partly it was curiosity. Partly it was a desire to escape his sister, if only for a few hours.

Taxi drivers in New Delhi are very familiar with the locations of cinema halls and temples. But Jag's three-wheeled taxi-scooter driver kept circling through a few potholed and dusty streets while the fare meter ran itself up. Jag was familiar with this sort of cheating and benevolently ignored it. Once the meter was high enough, the driver suddenly 'found' the small Shiv Temple he was looking for. Jag gave him an *I-know-you-are-cheating-me* smile when he paid the fare, but the driver showed no signs of guilt as he pocketed the extra money.

The old Pundit at the Shiv Temple immediately sensed that Jag was not a local, but a *foreign returned Indian*, an NRI. He greeted Jag with a smile reserved for big tippers. He produced a quick excuse when Jag enquired about the cause of his delay in finding a suitable match for Monica.

"Yes… Yes, I've been very busy. Do you know how hard it is to find suitable boys for such nice, sweet girls like your niece these days? All boys' mothers and aunts 'demand' so much now. God forbid; greed is overtaking this country." He paused to see Jag's reaction to his word 'demand.'

In an assertiveness training program in Toronto, Jag had been taught to deal with such people by showing no emotion. He used that training now, allowing no expression to cross his face, but the Pundit outpaced and outwitted him. Finally Jag tired of the stare-down and chose to wait no longer.

"Well, what have you got so far?"

With a big *I-got-you* smile on his face, the Pundit pulled out Monica's horoscope from a cloth bag and spread it out on a wooden table. Pointing to the zodiac circle on the horoscope, he said gravely, "Your very pretty and homely niece, Monica," he turned to look at the Shiv's statue as if asking for forgiveness for having to give such bad news to a rich client, then continued: "…is very unfortunately a Mangali."

Jag showed no shock. He leaned in closer, as though giving his full attention.

"Of course, this means she must marry a Mangali boy. Otherwise her stars would kill her husband." The Pundit shrugged and looked, dramatically, over at the statue once again.

Jag tried to simplify what was being imparted to him. "So, you're trying to tell me that Monica is born under the sign of Mangal which is bad, and we must find a match for her who is also born under the same sign, right?"

The Pundit nodded solemnly.

"So what's the problem? Let's find a Mangali boy!" Jag thought he had spoken the obvious. Problem solved!

The Pundit was ready. He was familiar with quick-solution answers from foreign returned Indians.

"Sir, it's not at all easy to find Mangali boys. There are many more Mangali girls than boys, thus the 'demand' is very high." He put special emphasis on the word 'demand,' so Jag would understand clearly the financial implications behind his words.

He waited patiently for an answer.

"Do you have any Mangali boys in your list right now, who might be suitable?" Jag tried not to show any impatience, but the Pundit was well versed with western *I-want-it-yesterday* attitudes.

He pulled out a small diary and flipped the pages back and forth uncertainly, and then announced, "I've this one. He's a good boy, an architect, same age as your niece. But your Number Two sister and brother in law may not like him."

Jag was a bit surprised, and asked why.

"We look for boys with good families. Good parents, the old folks still at home. This boy's parents died at an early age, when he was very young. His aunt brought him up. You know people here; they become suspicious for no reason. Like, maybe he has inherited some kind of disease from his parents and would die as soon as he is married," he answered diplomatically.

"What nonsense! When are people going to stop believing these old superstitions? Give me his name and address, and I'll personally go and check out this boy!" Jag's western self-righteousness jumped out, uncensored.

The old Pundit wrote down the boy's home and office address in Hindi on a small piece of paper, using both sides. "The boy's aunt may have a big demand, be careful. But the boy is ambitious and wants to immigrate to America. Maybe you can offer some help to him in this regard, and use this to bargain her down." He offered this insider's tip, passing over the paper.

Jag glanced at the paper and noticed that the Pundit's Hindi was very poor. He wondered how he managed to read horoscopes at all. When Jag looked up, he met the Pundit's eyes and saw they were full of expectation. Jag pulled out a twenty-Rupee bill and passed it to him, knowing in advance he would not accept such a small amount.

"Kya Sahib, you come from America and shame me with this twenty-Rupee note? I'm not a beggar! Even beggars get better than this."

The twenty Rupee bill went back into Jag's wallet and out came a fifty. He passed the bill to him and rushed towards the door before the Pundit could con him for any more.

"There will be more only after you get me some more names." He called out, over his shoulder, pleased with his quick exit.

Jag found Ajay, the boy from the Pundit's list, quite suitable for his niece Monica. He was ambitious and, yes, wanted to immigrate to America. He had already started to adopt western culture. To impress Jag, Ajay spoke mostly in 'Hindlish.' He was more than suitable. He was perfect. No parents, so fewer hassles of a joint family and lesser 'demands.' No typical everyday arguments with her mother-in-law for Jag's niece. And an added bonus was that he had inherited his parents' house too! Life would be a whole lot easier for a middle-class young couple in New Delhi. Ah, what a perfect match. Jag was pleased with the choice.

The biggest attraction, though, was the possibility of reducing the demand of a big dowry by dangling a carrot of immigration to Canada in front of Ajay. Jag felt he could wrap it all up in no time and was feeling proud of himself for having shown the benefits of western thinking and promptness in this old laid-back country.

Jag phoned Monica at her office and asked her to meet Ajay and him at the Hyatt Hotel after work. He cautioned her not to say anything to her mother. He wanted to prove to them that he could do things better and faster. He was excited for having set up the equivalent of, what they call in the West, a blind date for his favourite niece.

When Monica arrived Ajay promptly got up and said, "Hi," extending his hand to shake hers, showing that he was quite westernized. She politely put her hands up and said "Namaste," to prove she was very homely and still had Indian values. Jag chuckled, enjoying this Hindlish drama between the two.

The three had dinner at Hyatt's Tandoor. Jag was surprised to see Monica and Ajay mostly speak in Hindlish; half the sentences were in English and half in Hindi. After a respectable amount of time, Jag excused himself to go to the washroom and stopped at the bar next door. He celebrated by having a scotch with a beer chaser, proud of helping India shed some of its old-fashioned superstitious customs.

On the way home, in a three-wheeled scooter-taxi, Jag asked Monica "So, what do you think of Ajay?"

She politely answered, "He is okay."

Jag became overly excited about the possibility of a deal being struck so soon. "Should I go ahead and talk to his family? Do you like him?"

With no sign of emotion or excitement she answered politely again, "It's up to mom, dad and you. Whatever you think is right."

Jag was still high on his achievement. "O.K. Don't tell your mom and dad anything. I want to set this whole thing up and surprise them."

Monica nodded in a mute agreement.

The next morning, as usual, Jag's Number Two sister got out of bed after her husband and Monica left for work. She joined Jag, with her bed-tea, on the balcony where he was trying to find any bit of news about Canada in The Hindustan Times. Sitting on the cot in the sunshine, she put her one-armed eye glasses on and blurted out "Matrimonial?"

Jag passed her the advertisement section of the paper. After reading aloud a few of the matrimonial ads, she suddenly turned to face Jag.

"What did the Pundit say?"

Jag was very proud of his accomplishment in only one day, but kept any sign of excitement out of his voice. Sounding very serious, he said, "The Pundit says Monica is Mangali."

Jag's Number Two sister cried out. "What? Oh God no... No pundit had ever told us that before!"

Jag hadn't expected her to feel quite so strongly about this, for taking the blame so personally for Monica's being Mangali. He didn't want the scene to turn tragic.

"Well, this Pundit says Monica is actually a borderline Mangali. He showed me her horoscope. But at the same time he warned that families of suitable boys might consider her a full Mangali."

Despite his consoling voice, Jag could see the obvious pain on his sister's face, not just from realizing her only daughter was born Mangali, but that she was already thinking about all the future family accusations. Tears rolled down her face. "Are you sure?"

Jag wanted to lie but couldn't. "Yes, that's what the Pundit said."

His Number Two, tough and cantankerous, sister took off her one-arm eye glasses and buried her head in her sari, sobbing. Jag had never seen her like this before. She had always been his big sister. He couldn't control his inner excitement any longer.

"Now why are you crying and blaming yourself? I already have found a very good Mangali boy for Monica."

Still buried in her sari she warned Jag, "Don't joke with me. It's a serious matter to have Mangali daughters in India."

He could not hide the secret anymore, "No, I'm not joking. I did find a very good Mangali boy! In fact... In fact, I took Monica and him out for dinner last night, so both could meet each other."

Abruptly his Number Two sister jerked her face up from her sari.

"What do you mean you took Monica and him out for dinner?" Jag nodded, smiling broadly.

The tears stopped rolling out of her eyes as she asked, quite astonished, "But what about checking his horoscope, matching his stars with Monica's stars, and talking to his family - the 'demands' and all?"

Jag felt encouraged, "I thought they should meet each other first, and if they liked each other then we could proceed with all the formalities later."

His Number Two sister got up and went into the next room. After a few moments, Jag heard some noise. His curiosity got the better of him and he went to see what she was up to. He wasn't prepared for what he saw; his sister was throwing Jag's pack-sack and all his other things out of the door onto the hallway!

"What are you doing?" he screamed?

Without looking at Jag, with surprising politeness, she said, "We still live here in India, we've systems – matching stars! We've customs, of parents and relatives meeting first and negotiating a 'demand' before boy meets girl!" She grabbed Jag by the arm and walked him out into the hallway. "You can't just come back here and think you can run everything with your Canadian values!" She walked inside and slammed the door shut.

Jag's Number One sister wanted to know what had happened when he suddenly arrived at her door with all his luggage. Jag did not want to go into all the details just then, and so he simply said, "She threw me out."

She showed no surprise, when she asked, "Why?"

"I let Monica meet a suitable boy before telling her mother," Jag answered, the discomfort evident in his voice.

His Number One sister didn't speak for a few moments, then she turned to him and said quietly, "Ah, I don't think you would have done this if you were still living in India."

A few days later Jag wrote one line on a picture postcard and sent it to his Number Two sister.

"Yes! Mid-life crisis is an American disease!"

A BOLLYWOOD-STYLE LOVE STORY

Perhaps the scene might have gone something like this:

Number Two sister calls Number One sister after getting all the house chores done in the morning. She tells her the 'happy news' of Monica's forthcoming engagement, a relief after Jag's botched methods of trying to match up Monica with a suitable boy. Monica is finally going to get engaged properly! Number Two sister is very proud of her achievement, done without the help of Jag, her Canada-returned hippy brother. She now has bragging rights and wants to rub it in her younger brother's face. The Mr. Know-It-All!

The truth is that Number Two sister feels badly about throwing her younger brother out of her house, although she would never admit to this.

"We don't do such things in India, before all the arrangements are made," she had yelled at him before she slammed the door shut on him. Since then she has not called Number One sister to find out how Jag was taking her insult. So, after a week of guilt, Number Two sister decides to break the silence and calls Number One sister.

15

"He is not here now," she informs her slightly younger sister. "He has gone somewhere."

"Where did he go?"

Number One sister, who is getting hard of hearing, does not understand what Number Two is asking.

"He did not say much," she repeats herself. "Just going traveling. Searching for himself. Something like that. I did not understand him."

Number Two sister barks louder on the phone, thinking that perhaps Number One is not hearing properly. "Yes, he told me he has an American disease."

"What American?" Number One sister tries to turn off her hearing aid. It has started to buzz in her ear.

"He told me he has a mid-life crisis."

"What? Financial crisis?"

"Perhaps that too." Number Two sister had never thought of it. She thought that people who go to Canada swim in milk and honey. She continues in her loud bark, "In case Jag phones, you tell him that he must come back here for Monica's engagement next Monday. Or we will not talk to him ever again. She is his favourite niece!"

Number One sister smiles, for some reason she can hear better without the hearing aid. The smile has naughtiness in it. "He told me that he will never talk to you for rest of his life. You threw him out while he was trying to find a suitable boy for Monica."

Number Two will not take any blame in the family division. "He is our younger brother and once in a while we have a right to slap him if he gets out of line. Right?"

Number One nods and puts the phone down, thinking in her head that she has already said her good byes...

The above imaginary short film played out in Jag's mind, again and again, putting a smile on his face. It was easy for Jag to close his eyes in a crowded Indian train and lose himself in his imagination.

He loved both of his eldest sisters, but it had been almost sixteen years since Jag had moved to Canada, and much had changed for him. Or, at least, he had changed. He was no longer the young man who had once left, full of dreams and ambition. He was now a man in the beginning stages of a mid-life crisis. Jag could trace it back to the moment it had all started. His doctor had called him to tell him he had type two diabetes, and that he had no other choice than to suspend his pilot's license. His beautiful, successful life, as a pilot and owner of a small air charter business in northern Alberta, suddenly crashed like a doomed airplane. Feeling lost, he decided to pack everything and travel for a year. He thought it was a Canadian thing to do at forty! He arrived back in India with no plans. Now, all kinds of questions were being asked of him: "What are you doing? What's going on? What are your plans for the future?" He had not prepared any answers. For the first time in his life, he was a man with no answers. This was his mid-life crisis.

Perhaps he was back in India to find answers for his crisis, this American disease! But in India, when you return from abroad with no plan, you are considered a failure. And failed people have no respect in a middle-class society in his old country. Jag was reminded of this almost daily. One can behave like a hippy as long as one is rich. Poor India could tolerate the tantrums of rich NRIs - non-resident Indians - or foreigners, but had no time for returned failures.

When Jag wasn't pondering the question of success and failure, his mind drifted to other questions. Questions that pulled him back, like a grappling hook. Questions that had followed him to Canada and remained with him from the time he was a young man.

Of all the questions, there was one that seemed to be the answer to his journey: What happened to Francis?

Francis. Jag had met Francis in college when he was in first year. She had just finished her master's degree and the professors had liked her work so much that they hired her as a junior lecturer as soon as she graduated. She was four years older than Jag but, because of her young looks and petite size, she looked as if they both were equals. Besides, she still had not developed the seriousness of a lecturer. She behaved with her students as a classmate rather than a lecturer.

Jag felt Francis had an eye for him which helped him to improve his bravado. He was very proud of his looks and style. Besides, he was taking flying lessons, something that was sure to impress any woman. As a would-be pilot, Jag became a leader in the class. He was into drawings, photography and writing poems, the sorts of things to impress girls. But Jag did not fancy any of his classmates. He only wanted to impress Francis.

His friend, the editor of the monthly college magazine, agreed to print one of Jag's short poems - a *gazal*, an Urdu-style love poem - as a favor. This put Jag on the moon. He started to consider himself a literary scholar. Actually, he had done this after he had found out that Francis had an enormous interest in Hindi literature. She had done her M.A. in Psychology and minored in Hindi literature.

Jag started to carry the college magazine with the page open where his poem was published, hoping that he would run into

Francis in the college hallway. Deep in his mind he was hoping to impress, and perhaps develop some sort friendship with her. Dating was not popular in those days, and Patna was still a very backward city in the terms of western traditions and dating.

But Francis was not a typical Hindu girl. Her name was Francis Wheeler, from a converted Christian family, who were far more open and advanced than Hindus in India. Jag thought perhaps she might be more 'forward,' a word they used to give to people with western attitudes. She might be open to dating, being a Christian, even if he was younger than her. Jag built up these fantasies, dreaming more and more about Francis and himself. He became impatient with desire.

One day, while he was missing one of his 'boring' classes, Jag saw Francis walking alone in the hallway towards him. She was wearing a white and blue flowered cotton sari with the matching blouse. She wore no heels—just flat *chapels*. Her hair was done in a bun like a 1940s film star. A small black dot adorned her forehead. Jag thought her simplicity had elegance. She carried a small purse and a couple of books in her hands.

Jag walked straight to her. She sensed he wanted to talk to her so she stopped. She had a small but innocent smile - her way of greeting her students.

Jag pulled out the magazine from his books and, passing it to her, said, "Madam did you see my poem in this month's magazine?"

Francis did not take the magazine, her smile broadened and she nodded, "*Unha!*"

"What do you think?"

"It sounds like it's written by a sentimental young boy, not mature as a man yet. A boy does not understand what true love is."

Jag was not ready for such a quick and poignant critique. He was hoping she would be impressed and have kinder words, then he would pretend to be impressed by it and ask for another meeting or an appointment to discuss more literature with her. Perhaps this would allow their friendship to grow and, perhaps, in the future for them to date. Perhaps. Perhaps - maybe more perhaps later. He had hoped. But now it seemed all hope was gone. He felt he had demolished any chances of impressing Francis. He turned away with a very defeated face.

Francis noticed it. "Are you truly interested in literature?"

Jag couldn't talk, he was still choked up. He nodded. "*Unha.*"

"Then perhaps you should read some good Hindi literature, instead of the garbage. This will help you to grow up mentally." Then she paused and, with a smile, added slowly, "...and *physically.*"

"I am nineteen," Jag tried to make his voice sound manly.

Francis burst out laughing. "Yes, I know you are nineteen, but you are still a teenager. You need to read some good books and develop your taste. This will give you an insight into the human psyche." Passing a book to him, she continued, "Read this. It's an excellent book. I have read it. When you finish it, please return it to the library."

Jag glanced at the cover of the book: "*Gunaho Ka Devta*" by Dharamvir Bharati. He had never heard of the author, but the title thrilled him.

This thrill gave him confidence to ask, "Can I come and discuss this book after I have read it?"

"Sure, but first I want you to write me a one-page critique, after you have read it."

"This sounds more like a class assignment than a fun read."

"No, this is a learning exercise. If you want to understand good literature, then you have to work hard for it. What do you think, that fun is easy?" She gave him a naughty smile and walked away.

Jag did not feel discouraged with this encounter, despite her criticism of his poem, which he felt to be severe. He realized he might have to work hard to win her attention. He repeated her words in his mind, "What do you think, that fun is easy?"

In the next couple days Jag tried to read the novel. He was in a hurry to finish it. But he found it was so emotional that he could not go fast enough. The book made him think. He reread several paragraphs again and again. Eventually, he felt that he should slow down and perhaps make notes for the critique he would have to submit to Francis. He was used to reading thrillers and cheap spy novels, which came every month in a series. He could finish them in a day or two.

"*Gunaho Ka Devta*" was a different kind of book for Jag. It had a very rich text and the story was very emotional. He found his eyes filled up with tears in a few places while reading it. Jag had never felt so emotional reading a novel in the past. It took him almost a week to read the novel and, despite making some long notes from the book, he could not write a one-page critique on it. He felt he did not know enough to critique it. Jag felt helpless; never had a book in his past made him feel so inadequate. He could not write a poor critique and give it to Francis. That would completely ruin any impression he was hoping to make on her! He was afraid to face Francis. How was he going to tell her what he thought of the novel without sounding like a bumbling fool?

What to do? Jag was tormented between trying to impress Francis and not come across as 'not-mature-yet-as-a-man.' He wanted to win her somehow.

That same week, a new film, adapted from a very well-known Indian writer R.K. Narayan's book, *"The Guide,"* was released in town. It had huge publicity and the Indian public was very eager to see it. Jag somehow managed to advance-book two tickets for the next Saturday's matinee show. He made up his mind to ask Francis to see the film with him. Worst comes to worst, she would say no and, mentally, he could prepare himself for this possible rejection.

The next morning, wearing a nice and not-too-showy shirt, Jag walked into the shared office of lecturers. He found Francis sitting in one corner marking students' papers. Francis raised her eyes and smiled at him as if she was expecting him.

"So did you finish the novel?"

Jag nodded.

She continued, "And did you write me a one-page critique, as I had asked?"

"No, I am still writing it."

"How long it takes to write a one-page critique, for a poet like you?" She teased him.

Jag squatted next to her chair. Being a student, he was afraid to sit on the chair in the lecturers' office. This way he could talk to her in whispers.

"I found it very hard to read and write a critique. It's a very deeply emotional novel and it shattered me." Jag never thought he would be able to admit this to her so easily.

Francis noted the earnestness on his face. The naughtiness from her smile went away. She waited for Jag to speak out his feelings about the book.

"I'd like to sometime sit down and talk to you about this book. Perhaps try to understand it more."

Francis was very open, "Sure, we can meet here after the classes someday."

Jag blurted out, "I have two cinema tickets for the Saturday matinee of *"The Guide,"* made from R.K. Narayan's book. Would you like to come?" He wanted to make sure he said the writer's name slowly.

"Yes, it's made from R.K. Narayan's book but all you see is Dev Anand's face on the big posters. It must be a cheap Hindi version movie of his book. Do you know Narayan writes in English?"

Jag had never read R.K. Narayan and did not even know of any Indian writers writing in English. This was a second embarrassment, so quickly exposed in front of Francis.

"Do you want to read R.K.Narayan's book or do you want to see a Dev Anand film?" The naughtiness in her smile reappeared.

Jag got up from his squatting position and, giving up the idea of seeing the film with Francis, said, "Both, but with my college studies and my flying studies, I don't really have much time to read novels."

"Then perhaps you should switch one of your college subjects to literature, and," she paused to see his reaction, "you may have to stop watching these dumb Hindi movies."

Jag nodded. He had given up on the idea of her joining him for the film.

Francis continued, "So what time is the film?"

For the first time his face relaxed and he smiled back, "It's at 2:45 PM at Payal Cinema Hall on Saturday."

"OK, I'll see you there by the box-office," she whispered back.

Jag felt he was on a supersonic jet and left the room grinning. Saturday could not arrive soon enough.

Jag arrived early at the cinema hall. Although the tickets were for the first class and his seats were numbered, he still liked to get in early to sit down before the advertisements and trailers started. He wanted everything to be perfect and so he secured the seats because people often sat wherever they liked when it was crowded and then it was hard to move them in the dark. Sometimes arguments and yelling ensued while the usher tried to find alternative seats. Jag wanted to avoid any such scene with Francis coming in to see a film with him for the first time.

He kept pacing up and down by the box-office. A couple of scalpers tried to sell him black-market tickets. A few young men asked him if he had any spare tickets. This was the second weekend of the movie and it had quite a buzz. He started to worry; perhaps Francis had changed her mind and she was not coming. The cinema-hall's inside doors had been shut which meant they would be starting the trailers. He wondered if he should sell her ticket and head in. He did not want to miss the start of the film. Then he thought he would wait for seven more minutes before going in. Normally the commercials and trailers ran for about ten minutes.

Jag came out of the building to look for Francis on the road. On the other side of the street he saw her paying her rickshaw driver. He felt happy seeing her and waited till she crossed the road. She saw him and he waved at her.

"Did you get worried that I'd not come?" Her voice had that familiar teasing tone.

Jag could not quickly change his worrisome look but still he tried to pretend that he was nonplussed. "No, no. Let's go in; the trailers have started."

Jag tried to be polite and careful. He moved the black curtain for her so she could go in first. He whispered to her, "Let's wait till the usher comes with the torch."

People were in a rush to get to their seats and found Francis and Jag standing by the door a nuisance. A young man, seeing a young woman standing, tried to push Francis. Jag felt angry, but this was the way things happened in cinema-halls in small towns of India. Finally an usher showed up and Jag, showing his tickets, asked him to show them to their seats.

Fortunately nobody was sitting in their seats. Jag had reserved the corner seats so nobody would try to touch Francis in the dark. He let Francis sit in the corner seat and sat next to her in the row. He was being protective of her. He felt Francis could sense all his moves.

Finally, the movie! The noise calmed down. The opening credit song - *yehan kuan hain tera musafir, jayega kahan* by S.D. Burman - was very soothing. It almost lulled the crowd. The poet in Jag was touched by the lyrics. He relaxed and put his hands on the hand-rests. Francis's hand was already there. The touching sensation of her hand scared him and he pulled his hands down. He wondered if Francis was thinking he had put his hand to touch hers intentionally. This would make him look cheap, like those street ruffians who whistle at the passing girls.

Eventually the movie relaxed Jag and, from the corner of his eye, he could see Francis was enjoying it too. He noticed her smiling and even heard her laughing a couple of times. This made Jag happy.

When the movie ended, and the tail credits started to roll, people got into a big frenzy to get out. Francis whispered to Jag, "Let's not rush; let them get out then we will go out in peace. Ok?" Jag nodded and kept sitting in his seat.

He wanted to talk to Francis. How did she like the film, he wondered. He felt the film was well-made and quite literary. He asked her in whispers "Did you like the film?"

With her small smile, she said, "*Unha*. We will talk about in it detail when we get out of here."

Jag felt very happy to hear that. He would get a chance to talk to her privately, away from the college campus. He tried not to show his exuberance.

After a few minutes the crowd thinned out and Francis got up. Jag stayed right behind her so nobody would hit from the back or try to touch her bum. Francis liked Jag's protectiveness. She turned and smiled at him. Slowly they walked out of the theatre.

The sun was just starting to set. The sky in the west was quite red. The light powder makeup on Francis's face was still hanging on, despite a few sweat drops on her face. Jag noticed that the blouse under her armpits was wet. She looked very nonchalant about the whole thing. It did not bother her that Jag's eyes were examining her.

"Can I invite you for an ice cream or an espresso coffee? There is a very nice restaurant called The *Kwality*, close to here." Francis suggested.

"Certainly. I have come on my scooter, would you like to ride with me? Hope you are not scared of scooters?"

Francis nodded and followed him to the stand. She watched him kick-start his scooter and then sat on the back seat. She put her hand on his shoulder to hold tight to him, and moved her body closer on the scooter's seat.

Suddenly the blood surged in Jag's body. He let the feeling sink in. This was his dream come true!

"Is The *Kwality* opposite the Gandhi Maidan?" He asked over the sound of the scooter's engine.

Francis did not want to scream over the scooter noise so she brought her lips very close to Jag's ears and said, "Yes," and, in doing so, Jag could feel her breast touching his back. The excitement of her touch put Jag over the moon. He felt adrenaline surge through his body. Jag was not religious, but he prayed to God, in his mind, "Please help me not to make a fool of myself with this woman."

At the restaurant, Francis suggested a quiet, corner table.

"Since you bought the film tickets, this will be my treat. No arguments." Francis said very firmly.

Jag gave a noncommittal nod. He ordered an Indian espresso, which was like a French Latte, and she ordered a three-in-one ice cream. Jag wanted to seem like a western-style bohemian. He thought ordering an espresso was perhaps bohemian but worried she might think it may be bourgeois. He had read these big words in English but was not quite sure what they exactly meant. He thought he should use the words in their conversation. He wanted to sound cool.

It was Jag's first time in a westernized restaurant and he was a bit uncomfortable, although he tried to conceal it. Francis's comfort level in the restaurant gave him an indication that she had been there a few times. He wondered if she came alone or not.

Francis watched his expression for a few minutes. There was an awkward silence between the two. She knew it was the moment to change the student-teacher relationship into an adult friendship but she wondered how she should start. Finally, she asked, "What sort of problems did you have following the novel *Gunaho Ka Devta*?"

Jag jumped in as if he was ready for such an opening question. "First the name - *Gunaho Ka Devta* - God of Crimes or God of Mistakes, is a bit of a strange title. It's sort of a self-contradictory title."

"Oxymoron title," Francis interrupted.

"What?" He did not understand the word.

"Look it up in the dictionary. Let's continue with your self-contradictory title."

Jag paused to recollect his thoughts. Her interruption had broken his chain of thoughts. He looked around to see if the waiter was coming. There was no sign of him. He did not want to be interrupted again.

"You see," he put both his elbows on the table and moved forward towards her so he could talk to her in a lower voice. "One cannot be a god of crimes for loving somebody so furiously. Love is not a sin. Love is not a crime. Love is not a mistake. But the writer has called his hero..." Jag could not remember the word protagonist, "... a God of Crimes for pure love. It's not right. No, it's not right."

Francis smiled at his conviction, when he repeated his line a second time. She felt she was destined to make a mature thinking man out of this sentimental young boy. Perhaps she could teach him what pure love is. The thought brought an enigmatic smile to her lips.

Francis's smile frustrated Jag.

"What?" He asked.

Francis continued to smile. "Perhaps you have never experienced true love, or you have never loved somebody so fiercely that you find it to be a sin, or a crime. Not to others but to your own soul."

Jag was lost. He wondered, "How can loving somebody be a sin to your own soul?"

Silence hung in the air between them. Francis purposely left this silence lingering, thinking she had made this young man wonder or, perhaps, made him curious to reflect on the nature of love.

Jag finally broke the silence. "I think I have to mull this over and maybe read the book again."

"Good. When you reflect on a novel with a rational thought process, you learn more about the characters, because they speak to you. You learn more about yourself by wondering what if you were that character." Francis spoke as if she was in a class.

"I guess then we can meet more often and talk about it?" Jag was happy that this would give him more chances to develop his relationship with her.

Francis was straight forward in her answer. "Certainly, as long we share our expenses. You are a student and I am a lecturer and I earn and you don't."

Jag was familiar with this sharing of costs with his male friends, but sharing with a woman, especially the one he was becoming fond of minute by minute, was a blow to his male ego. He wanted to object but, realizing Francis's firm attitude about it, did not risk it. Instead he made fun of it and teased, "You are taking away a man's privilege by proposing such an arrangement."

Francis was quick, "Get off from your high horse, Jag. You are just a boy, not even a man yet. When you grow to be a man, I may consider your privilege." Her smile almost turned into a giggle.

Jag enjoyed this. "Yes, Madam."

Jag was thrilled when Francis agreed to ride at the back of his scooter when he offered her a lift to the Teacher's Hostel. She sat at the back seat with her hand on Jag's shoulder, again. Jag was conscious of her touch and his blood started to run at twice the speed. He drove slowly to make it last as long as possible. He was very careful not to scare Francis with any rash driving. He stopped at the Hostel's gate. Francis wanted to walk inside alone so as to not attract any attention from other lecturers. She spoke quietly. "I enjoyed the evening. Thank you."

She was ready to turn and walk inside the gate, when Jag asked, "Can we continue this sort of conversation every weekend?"

Francis expected this question and smiled when it popped up. "Sure, as long as I have nothing else planned." She did not wait for Jag's answer and walked away.

*****

Jag opened his eyes. He had been lost in thoughts of his past. The train was stopped at a small station. A man was trying to climb in the train compartment with a huge basket of live chickens on his head. The basket was bigger than the door, but he somehow pushed through it. A man from inside helped him pull it into the compartment. Jag watched the whole drama from his corner seat, amused. He had never, not even once, seen anything like this in all his years in Canada. The chickens' smell bothered him but, when he looked around, he saw that he was the only one bothered by it.

Jag closed his eyes again and tried to go back to his nostalgic thoughts but it was like waking up in the middle of a dream. He could not remember the details of how his relationship developed with Francis over three years while he finished his university and flying lessons. Everything started to move in fast-forward motion. Their relationship had slowly changed from literary-platonic to emotional-sexual. He became saturated with literature, even tried to write some short stories and poems.

Francis started to see their life together in future terms while Jag was thinking of going abroad. He could not foresee a career for himself in India. He moved back home, away from the college and secretly applied for government grants to go abroad for helicopter training. He did not have much hope but he pursued his dream anyhow. His eyes had been opened to possibility and Jag wanted to experience the world.

Then one day he got two letters: The first was from Reserve Bank of India, approving his trip to Canada for helicopter training; he would have to leave within 30 days. The second letter was from Francis. A one-line letter reading: *I need to see you urgently.*

Jag was in a rush to get everything ready for his new chapter in his life. He needed his visa from the Canadian Embassy, his airline ticket, arrangement for the money to be transferred to him and all other things when one has to get ready for study abroad. Jag's family was not very happy about his leaving. His mother went into a depression. His father asked him to reconsider. But Jag continued with his plans. He felt he couldn't live in India anymore. There was so much more to see and experience.

He wrote a short letter to Francis saying that he would stop by for a short visit on the way back from Delhi. He did not tell her that he was getting ready to leave for Canada.

Fortunately for Jag, everything at the embassy went well and he got his student visa in just three days. He took the train back to Patna, where Francis still lived. She was not at the train station to meet him. He got worried, despite his personal enthusiasm of going abroad.

When he arrived at Francis's house, she looked drawn and tired. But Jag chose to ignore it. He was bubbling over with news about forthcoming his trip to Canada. He told her everything in

31

a hurry, full of excitement, and then he realized Francis was not, in any way, sharing his enthusiasm.

"What's the matter?"

"Jag, I am pregnant."

It hit Jag like an electric shock; he felt dumbfounded. He never thought something like this would happen, especially when he was ready to go abroad. He barely could speak but somehow managed to fumble a few words. "Now? When I am going to leave?"

"You tell me what do you want to do? Do you want to get married in a court or do you want me to abort it?" Francis's words were very precise, as if she already knew what Jag's answer would be.

Both their families were against their relationship. Francis was older than Jag and a Christian by religion, which was not acceptable to his family. Even Francis's brother and aunt had opposed her relationship with Jag. He had never worked. He had been a student either at university or at the Flying School. He might have a bright future but presently he was unemployed.

"I feel I should stand on my own two feet, before I marry you. You, at least, have a job but I have nothing." He looked to Francis for understanding. Her face was blank, unreadable. He could not understand what she must have been going through. To be pregnant before marriage was almost a sin! The society totally disapproved of it and usually it was only women who were harshly judged.

"Fine. Let's find a doctor who can do this as soon as possible. Can you stay for a couple of days?" Francis's tone was very dry and clinical. Jag nodded.

In the afternoon, Jag was able to arrange an illegal abortion with a government employed lady-doctor on the condition that he must take Francis away from her clinic right after the procedure.

The next morning the doctor did the procedure. It was fast, over with in less than twenty minutes. She then suggested that Jag should take Francis home to let her rest for a couple of days.

Jag paid the doctor and she gave him a small paper bag. Inside was the fetus. He did not know what to do with it. In a panic he threw it off the balcony, into a garbage dump below. But the image of the fetus was engraved into his mind.

Francis looked pale but she was able to move around a little bit. He brought her home in a rickshaw. She was in pain and bleeding slightly but nothing seemed to be scary or dangerous.

To erase the image in his mind he thought of his trip to Canada. He was careful not to say much, but it seemed Francis was able to read his thoughts. By the evening, Francis told him to leave and go to Calcutta in order to prepare for his Canada trip. He suggested that he should stay for at least one more day till she was a bit stronger but she insisted, saying that she would be fine. He left for Calcutta that night.

Jag did not hear anything from Francis for almost two years. He wrote several letters to her from Canada, but never got any replies. He mostly told her about the difficulties of his training, being short of money and not being able to find any work immediately - the usual struggles of a new immigrant. He did not want to return to India as a failure or poor. He knew it would take him a long time to establish himself in Canada before he could bring Francis over and marry her. Away from the disapproval of their families.

Soon the new country, the new ways, all the new attractions combined with no communication from Francis, made Jag forget about his feelings for her. Some of the white girls' attraction was helping him to forget her. But something still nagged him from time to time and he knew that he had left many things undone. He decided to write one of the Francis's friends, Kamala, to find out about her. He had never discussed their relationship with anybody, but he wanted to find what was in Francis's heart and mind so that he could move on. Guilt was prohibiting him from fully embracing his new life.

After a few weeks he received a very long letter from Kamala. He knew Kamala was a drama queen, and she always loved telling everything in great detail. He summarized Kamala's letter in a few sentences: Francis had fallen very sick at the time he left for Canada and she spent a long time in a hospital. She did not want Jag to know about this. She was back at work and, right now, her family was trying to arrange a wedding for her.

Jag felt sad with the news. He did not acknowledge or thank Kamala for her prompt answer. He decided to forget about everything and bury his past with Francis. He would erase her memory from his mind. But still, sometimes, somewhere, a lingering guilty feeling would pop up uninvited and it haunted him.

Surprisingly, soon after; he received a very short letter from Francis, after almost two years' wait. She wrote, "My family wants me to get married. They have chosen a suitable boy for me. My father is very ill and old. He would like to see me married before he passes away. Should I wait for you? Please tell me."

Normally, Jag would have started writing a response immediately but this time he waited, unsure of what to say. He felt he should let Francis be free to choose for herself. Besides, he was very insecure about his present life. He was struggling within Canada. This was not a land of milk and honey for him, not the way he had dreamed it would be while he was still in India. At least, not yet. But he just couldn't bring himself to explain his struggles to her in a letter.

Finally he wrote back, "I am not worth waiting for. Right now, I will not even wait for myself. Please go ahead with your family's arrangement. Have a happy life. Good luck. Please let me know if I can do anything for you."

The answer from her came very quickly this time. The letter hadn't the least sentimentality or romantic nostalgia. It was, again, a very short letter. Francis had written, "Thank you. Yes, you can do something for me. I'd like you to send me a white wedding veil suitable for a bride. I want your veil on my head when I am getting married. This will be my goodbye to you."

Jag could not control his tears and cried after reading the letter. He went with a female friend to The Bay to buy a beautiful veil. He spent more than he could afford. Now he had credit cards. "Buy now and pay later" - Jag was learning the American way. He put a small note on the veil, "Please send me a photograph." He packaged it very safely and mailed it, with express and registered delivery to Francis.

He never heard back from Francis. No wedding photographs came. A year later his mangled package came back with a note from the post office: Send back to the Sender. Addressee not found. Inside, the veil was broken and his note was still there. Jag controlled his tears this time and accepted his fate like the returned broken veil...

****

The train started to slow down. This time, when Jag opened his eyes, they were wet. The train stopped at the station where he was supposed to get off. He took his little bag and slowly made his way to the door. As he got off the train, he asked himself if he really was ready to find out: "What happened to Francis?"

When Jag got off, after jumping over the chicken basket by the door, the train had already started to move again. On these small stations the trains hardly stop for a minute or two. There were no rules who boards first or who gets off first. It's always a big push of people coming and going. Jag pressed through at the last minute and jumped to the platform. He had never come to this village by train before. It looked so different from everything he remembered from twenty years ago.

Jag had once brought Francis's older brother, Alex, to the village from Patna. Alex had become very ill during the summer holidays when Francis had gone to their village home. Jag had gone to see Alex, the only member of Francis's family who liked Jag and was not in opposition to their relationship. As soon as Jag walked into his flat, he saw Alex sitting on his cot, puking blood onto the floor. Jag got very worried and immediately called a doctor for a house call. The doctor told him that perhaps Alex had caught T.B. He should be taken to a hospital for more tests, and he should be on total rest. Jag asked the doctor if he could take Alex to his village home where all his family lived and where he would be well taken care of. The doctor prescribed some medicines and wrote a short letter for the village hospital. Jag was torn between worry for Alex and excitement about going to Francis's village home. He had never been there and he had not seen her for over a month.

Jag did not want to take any chances. In those days there was no bridge over the river Ganges, so people crossed it in ferries and then caught the trains to their final destination. He took a taxi from the ferry site to Francis's village home. Alex was objecting to Jag's spending so much money on him. He mildly protested by saying he'd be able to travel by train. But Jag did not listen to him. He wanted to make sure Alex arrived at his home in all the comfort.

When Jag arrived at the village home with Alex, Francis opened the door. She only saw Jag's back as he was helping Alex out of the taxi. She wondered why Jag would come to visit her in a taxi. Then she saw him helping Alex out of the car and she ran towards them. They did not talk; they just helped Alex inside the house. Soon all other members of the family gathered around. They looked at Jag knowingly but did not acknowledge him. Jag understood their coldness, despite the good deed he had done for Alex.

He came outside on the porch to wave to the taxi driver, letting him know he should wait a few more minutes as he had hired him for a return trip. Francis followed him out. He handed her all Alex's medicine, the prescription, and the letter for the hospital.

"The doctor thinks Alex has T.B. He needs a lot of tests and rest." Jag wanted to touch Francis concerned face but he did not. Being an Indian, he knew the protocol of such a situation. She nodded. Jag headed for the taxi. He heard Francis's whisper, "I'll see you in Patna soon. Bye."

Jag turned and looked at her. Her lips were pursed with a contained smile. He jumped into his waiting taxi. Francis stayed in the porch till the taxi was out of her sight.

On the way back, the student pilot Jag made a mental map of the road and location just in case if he would ever have to go there again…

Now, at the same railway station almost twenty years later, Jag was trying to recall the map from his memory. The sun was almost in the middle of the sky, trying to heat up. The crowd was no different than any other towns and villages Jag had visited in the past. He did not feel like a stranger here. He looked around for an old rickshaw-wala driver who may remember things from twenty years ago. Seeing one he walked up to him.

Jag asked him, "Do you know *Mithanpura*—the water-tank tower?"

The old rickshaw-wala driver did not answer him right away. He was trying to measure Jag up. Was he a local? Or an Indian from another state or an Indian from out of country? Rickshaw-walas quote a fare only after figuring this out from the accent of the passenger. Finally he spoke, "I know *Mithanpura*, but I have to ask about the water-tank tower there."

Jag sat on his rickshaw and ordered him, "*Chalo*," - let's go, without bargaining for a fare. The rickshaw-wala understood this man was from outside and he'd be paid a better than fair fare.

It did not take long for the rickshaw-wala to reach *Mithanpura*. Jag could see the water tower from a distance and pointed it out to him. The words *Mithanpura* had faded from the tower, but were still readable. A lot more houses were built now than twenty years ago. Most gravel roads were paved. The place looked more like a small town than a village. Jag was not sure if he would be able to find Francis's house in this crowded place. He asked the rickshaw-wala to take him under the water-tank tower. He remembered it was around four in the afternoon when the taxi had turned on the gravel road from the tower on Alex's instruction. The sun had hit him on his face. He figured if he took a westbound road from the tower then he should be able to find her house. Flying in northern Canada had improved Jag's navigation methods. But when he figured out west from the tower, he found three streets instead of one, and all paved. No gravel street. Jag tried to remember any other signs, but nothing came to his mind. He decided to take a chance and asked the rickshaw-wala to take the middle street. He remembered the house was very close to the tower and on the right side of the street going in.

There was a big iron gate and a garden in the front of the house. He remembered seeing Francis's father's name plate on the gate, a style Indians had inherited from the British. Having worked with the British, and being a Christian, Francis's father had a western influence on his lifestyle. Though Jag's family was richer, but not as advanced in western styles as Francis's family was, this had once given him an inferiority complex.

Jag felt happy with this sudden memory and was sure now he would be able to find the house. He was right and lucky. Barely had the Rickshaw-wala driven for 3 minutes before he saw Mr. Wheeler's name plate on the old iron gate. He asked the Rickshaw-wala to stop and wait for him there. The iron gate had rusted and was barely hanging on its hinges on one side. The garden was dry from negligence and outside walls were faded with paint peeling. The bungalow looked dilapidated. Jag walked in slowly and knocked on the door.

After waiting a few minutes, the door opened. It was Fred, Francis's younger brother who did not like or approve of Jag. Jag recognized Fred right away, but he was not sure if Fred would recognize him; Jag had gained weight and was no longer a young man.

"I am Jag Mohan." He offered, hoping he would be invited in to talk politely. After all, it had been at least twenty years.

Fred said dryly, "Yes I recognize you. What can I do for you?" He did not invite Jag inside the house.

Jag was not sure how to ask him about Francis. He looked around. He saw his Rickshaw-wala had parked under a tree and was ready to go for a short snooze. Then he turned to Fred's stern face, "I am trying to find Francis. Can you tell me where I can find her?"

"No. Don't you think you have caused her enough harm?"

Jag was not sure about Fred's insinuation. But he did not want to argue this at his door. Jag had mastered his politeness in Canada. "I have traveled a long distance to come here. From Canada," to emphasize both the distance and the fact that he now lived abroad, thinking perhaps this may impress him. "Can you at least tell me how Alex is, and his address?"

Fred was not impressed. "Alex is fine. He is retired now and living in Patna. Wait, I'll write down his address for you."

Jag still did not get invited in. Fred returned in a few moments with a small piece of paper with Alex's address.

Jag wondered if he should leave a message for Francis in case he could not find Alex in Patna, or could not meet Francis. But seeing Fred's face, he chose not to. He said "thank you" to him and walked back to his rickshaw. He felt some eyes were watching him from behind the window curtains. Jag felt lousy with Fred's treatment and thought maybe he should give up trying to find Francis. Let the past be past.

He sat in the rickshaw and told the driver, "*Chalo wapas,* station." - back to the train station.

Rickshaw-wala wiped his face with his sleeve and started to pedal slowly.

Jag looked at Alex's address on the small piece of paper. This seemed to be a new area in Patna. He couldn't remember it from his flying training days. He thought again about whether he should try to find Alex in Patna or fly back to Delhi to be present at his favourite niece Monica's engagement party the next evening. He knew if he did not make it for the party, his Number Two sister would be very angry with him. And worse, Monica would be hurt.

A voice in his heart told him, "But you traveled two thousand kilometers to find Francis and see what happened to her, and now you want to give up? You knew well that her family members do not like you except Alex, so you should have been prepared for it." The voice of his heart won. He decided to go to Patna and look for Alex and to find Francis. He knew Alex would have told him what happened to Francis and where she is now. Besides, he had to go to Patna to catch his flight for Delhi. Excuse found - mind settled.

"Do you have an idea when is the next train for Patna?" He asked the rickshaw-wala.

"In about an hour," Rickshaw-wala answered him from his sweaty face. Jag did not see any watch on him, so he wondered how he knew about the time. But he knew this was India and people had their own way of knowing the time.

"And how long will it take to get to the station?" Jag asked again.

Rickshaw-wala was out of his breath with the heat and pedaling, but he did answer Jag, "Way before your train comes in."

Jag noticed that it was difficult for the old driver to pedal in this heat and talk to him at the same time. So he decided to shut up. He closed his eyes and tried to snooze in the slow-moving rickshaw. Surprisingly, with all this heat and noise, he did fall into a deep sleep.

"*Hazoor,*" the Bihari word for Sir, and a light touch of Rickshaw-wala's hand on his knee woke him up.

Jag got off the rickshaw. "Do you think the train has come?"

"Naw. Still lots of time."

Jag noticed the full sweaty face of the rickshaw-wala. The man was not old, but the life had made him look very old. Jag passed him a one hundred-rupee note, and waited to see him smile. The old-looking man did not smile but put both hands in *pranam* to him and said, "God will bestow happiness on you."

"Really?" Jag smiled at him then winked and headed for the ticket booth. He did not want to hear anything more for his generosity.

By the time he arrived at Patna, the sun had set. The streets looked foggy in the dim lights. But in reality it was pollution that made the city look so bleak. He checked into a small hotel near the station. He found from the reception that there were two flights to Delhi in the morning—one direct and other via Lucknow; same two in the evening. The flights originated from Calcutta.

It did not take Jag long to find Alex's flat. But Alex was not home and his Nepali maid was not sure what time he would return, but she offered for him to wait in the drawing room. Canadian Jag was quite surprised with her trust with an unknown man. The maid was extremely polite. She brought him a very sweet milky chai tea and some biscuits. He could not drink the tea but he ate a couple of biscuits.

Jag thought of chatting with the maid. "So what time does Alex come home?"

"Late. Sometimes at 11:00, sometimes at 11:30. He eats then and goes to sleep." She nodded her head from side to side. She still had a heavy Nepali accent. She must be new in India, Jag thought.

She felt encouraged to talk to him. "Where do you come from? Delhi?"

Jag enjoyed her accent and did not mind talking to her to pass the time. "Right now I have come from Delhi, but I live very far."

"Where?"

"Canada."

"Ka-na-da. Where is that in south India?"

Jag smiled because there is a language in south India which has similar pronunciation as Canada only spelled as Kannada.

"No this is a country very far from here—it's on the other side of the sea."

She nodded again as if she understood him.

"So how long you have been working here?"

She put two fingers up.

Jag asked again, "Two months?"

She shook her head no, and added, "years," and nodded to him to confirm Jag understood it was two years and not two months.

Jag smiled broadly. "Two years - not two months. Right?" He mimicked her nodding. She smiled and nodded yes to him this time.

"Where is your luggage? You are going to stay here tonight, right?"

"No, I am staying in a hotel. I am flying early in the morning." Jag liked her simple directness.

"So soon. You should stay here for a few days with us. What's the hurry? After how many years you are visiting Sahib?"

"Almost twenty years."

"*Bap-re* twenty years. I wonder if sahib would recognize you."

Jag wanted to laugh out loud at her exclamation of *Bap-re*, an expression like *Oh my God.* But he controlled it with a small smile.

"Do you know sahib's family - his brother or sisters?" Jag tried to find any information from her about Francis.

"Nobody visits from sahib's home. He does not go either. He lives mostly alone." She felt sad for Alex's loneliness.

Jag decided not to probe her any further, and kept quiet. She picked up the dishes and headed for the kitchen. "I better cook sahib's dinner. You are staying for the dinner at least, yes?"

Jag unwillingly nodded yes to her. Suddenly, he felt he wanted quiet. After she left the room, he closed his eyes and tried to have a snooze. It did not take him long to start snoring. He did not hear when Alex came in. It was only when Alex entered the room that Jag awoke.

Alex looked the very same as twenty years ago, except for a few grey hairs. He did not have any sign of a man who had suffered from T.B. twenty years earlier. But Alex did not recognize Jag. Jag was a young man last time Alex saw him. Now Jag was a middle-aged man with a lot more weight around his waist. But when Jag told him his name, he was happy to see him and hugged him as a lost relative.

The maid started to set up the dinner for both men. Alex looked at her and understood that Jag would be staying for dinner. He excused himself and went to the washroom to freshen up.

Jag wondered how he should ask Alex about Francis. Suddenly he felt uneasy about his coming here. Both sat down for dinner while the maid stood in the corner watching them. Alex started to mix in his rice and lentil with his fingers, the Indian way. Jag could not do it, and asked the maid for a spoon. She rushed back with one, wiping it with her fingers. Jag looked at it to make sure it was clean.

"So how is your family? You have a wife and kids?" Alex started, saving Jag the problem of asking further questions. He did not know how to tell Alex that he had been to his village home and his younger brother refused to tell him Francis's whereabouts.

"No family."

Alex gave him a *what-do-you-mean* look. Jag continued, "No girl ever proposed to me. I never married." Jag tried to make the atmosphere lighter.

Alex smiled at his answer. "Nobody told you men do proposing?"

"I see you have stayed a bachelor too."

"I had never planned to marry. Now that I have a nice maid, I don't need a wife. So how do you manage? Who does your cooking and cleaning?" Alex's curiosity grew.

"It's easier in Canada to do all this on your own. You have washing machines for dishes and clothes. And cleaning house is not all that hard." Jag found himself staring at the way Alex was licking his fingers and enjoying his meal.

"And you are still piloting?"

"No."

The question mark showed up on Alex's face again.

"I am medically grounded. I have type two diabetes. So they took away my pilot's license."

Alex tried to understand what all this meant, then Jag slipped in his question, "How is Francis? Where is she?"

"She is fine. She works in a Government Central School as a teacher. She just adopted a baby girl last year. Her husband is a very nice man, a bit older than her, but a gentleman."

"Adopted? Why?" It worried Jag.

"Oh you know, she had some medical problems, just when you departed for overseas. Now she cannot conceive."

The news bothered Jag. Was he responsible for that misfortune, he wondered.

"They are a very happy family. Aunty is with them. She is helping Francis to bring the baby up, when she goes to teach."

Jag could not eat any more. He kept playing with his rice with his spoon.

"Where does Francis live?" Finally he had gathered enough courage to ask.

"They live in Lucknow. She has a nice government quarters in the school's compound. They have a nice lifestyle."

Jag dared more, "Do you think it'd be okay for me to visit her? Or would it cause her problems?"

"Sure, sure. She would be happy to see you again after all these years. Like I said her husband is a very nice guy."

"Does she have a phone at home?"

"No, you can't have a phone on a teacher's salary here. It's not like your rich Canada here." Alex smiled, "You must have saved up a bundle by now!"

Jag smiled back, "No. It takes a long time to settle in Canada, and then I had to pay back all my Helicopter training student loan. I am almost back to zero now with my pilot's license suspended."

Alex was surprised with Jag's honest confession of his poverty. Indians, especially foreign returned Indians, do not say such things so openly. He did not know how to respond to Jag's confession.

Jag saved him, "I am thinking of going back to Canada to start a new career; maybe go back to a college and learn a new thing. You know it's very common for people in Canada to do this. People go for re-training at the age of forty and fifty."

Alex laughed. "Can they retain the new things they learn at that age?"

"I hope so." Jag looked at the maid and told her, "I can't eat any more. I am not used to eating so late. I am full now."

Alex went to the kitchen and washed his hands in the sink. Jag did not feel any need to wash his hands, as he had used the spoon.

The maid spoke gently as she picked up his plate, "You hardly ate. Perhaps you did not like my cooking."

"I was not very hungry and you gave me too much." Jag tried to find an excuse.

She smiled at his lie and went into the kitchen. Jag knew she understood his lie. These unspoken understandings were part of the Indian customs and everybody accepted it without much fuss.

Jag looked at Alex obligingly. There was no anger like Fred's on his face. Jag wanted to ask more about Francis's adoption of a baby girl, but he could not dare any more. He was afraid of some unsaid things. He thought, 'Let the unsaid things stay unsaid.'

Jag asked for his leave; he told Alex he had to catch an early morning flight for Delhi as his favourite niece was getting engaged the next day, and he must attend the ceremony. The good-byes with Alex were polite and warm. He forced some Indian Rupees in the maid's hand, despite her protests.

In the early morning Jag called for a taxi to the airport, instead of a rickshaw. He had to book the tickets to Lucknow and then to Delhi on the evening flight from there. He was excited and nervous. Would he be able to see Francis and make it to Delhi all in one day? He was truly becoming a jet-setter in India, which was an uncommon word there amongst his family and friends. He knew nobody would believe his efforts to find Francis; for them it would be a Bollywood film story Jag had made up.

The minute the taxi got out of the city on the way to the airport, Jag's heart sank. As he got closer to the airport the fog got thicker. The pilot in Jag knew that the airport was not equipped with an instrument landing system and most junior pilots of Indian Airlines were not trained to land in such thick fog. Although an atheist, Jag prayed in his heart that the fog would lift soon.

At the airport, except for the staff, there was nobody. Most of them were having their tea break, as nothing was going to happen any time soon in the heavy fog. They were used to such delays. After a lot of shouting by Jag, "Hello, hello? Is anybody here?" A short, middle-aged man in the Indian Airlines uniform showed up with an expression of why-are-you-yelling and, before Jag could say a word, he said in a Bengali-accented English, "All flights are delayed due to fog." He was ready to turn back and go to his tea.

"Yes, but I want to buy my tickets." Jag spoke hurriedly in his Hindilish, before the man was gone.

"Now? Can't you wait till we know what time the flight is coming?"

"Please, yes now, it will be crowded later and I don't want to be fighting with the crowd. Please *dada*." Jag added the Bengali word *dada* as a token respect for him. The man gave him an unhappy look and pulled a huge big ledger type of book from under the counter. The computerized booking was not yet introduced in Indian Airlines and they had a monopoly in the country. No private airlines were allowed in India at the time.

"I need a ticket from here to Lucknow on the morning flight and Lucknow to Delhi in the evening flight." Jag requested.

The agent did not bother to acknowledge Jag's request and continued to look over the big ledger. Jag could not understand how he figured out the number of seats available. He felt he had better stay quiet and not annoy this agent any more.

The agent went back and forth on different pages of the big ledger, and finally looked up. "Yes, you can have seats. Are you a foreigner?"

"I am an Indian, living abroad." Jag answered, sensing problems. He was sure he would find a way to settle it, after all, this was his home turf and he had trained at this very airport as a pilot.

"Do you have and Indian passport or a foreign passport?"

"A Canadian passport."

"Then you have to pay 30% more for your tickets. NRI have to pay same as foreigners," the agent explained, expecting an angry outburst from Jag. Mostly Indian men feel cheated when they find out they have to pay more than others.

"Fine!" Jag gave a short answer.

The agent started to write and then paused. "Do you have your passport with you sir?"

"No, I don't travel in my own country with the passport." Jag emphasized.

"But, Sir, you are not an Indian, you are a foreigner. And we must check the passports of all foreign citizens."

Finally, Jag lost his temper. He switched from his Hindilish to Canadian accented English and yelled, "Nobody has ever challenged me or asked me for my passport before. I have traveled here so many times."

"Fine sir, I am not challenging you, I am just telling you the rules." The authority in the agent's voice popped up.

"May I speak with the Airport Manager?" Jag tried to be calm.

"He is perhaps in the control tower, but he has nothing to do with the airline." The authority stayed in the agent's voice.

Jag rushed up to the tower. He knew this airport well from his training days, and nothing seemed to have changed since then.

Bharat, like so many of Jag's classmates who could not find piloting jobs, had become an air-traffic controller. During their training days, Jag did not like him; Bharat was junior to him in training, and he was a loud mouth. But right now, Jag had to forget the past. He needed a favour from him. He patted on his shoulder from behind to surprise him.

Bharat turned and immediately got up to hug him, "Boss, when did you come here? This is really a pleasant surprise. Sit. Sit." Bharat spoke in his Bihari Hindi from the training days; then he turned and shouted to the office peon, "Bring a chair for Jag sahib. Quick." In the meanwhile, he offered his own chair to Jag. Jag noticed Bharat's name tag on his shirt, 'Dy - Aerodrome Officer.' He smiled at Bharat.

Two junior controllers were curiously looking at Jag. Bharat noticed it and gave them a very boasting introduction of Jag, "He and I did our flying training here together. Now he is flying water bombers and helicopters in Canada."

No names were mentioned in introductions. The two junior controllers were suitably impressed and nodded to Jag. He returned their nod in respect.

Jag looked around; nothing had changed since his student pilot days. He looked at Bharat and said, "It looks so much the same."

"Oh, we have a couple of new instruments, nothing more."

The peon brought a chair for Jag and offered it to him.

"Go get some special tea for Jag sahib!" Bharat ordered.

Jag wanted to get to the point right away. He did not want to get caught in the Indian formalities. He was unable to relax; he wanted to be sure he would have the tickets to travel. He couldn't afford to miss the flight and not find Francis or miss Monica's engagement.

"I need a big favour from you. The IA clerk downstairs is refusing to sell me tickets to Lucknow and continue to Delhi this evening. He says I must show him my passport, being a foreigner, and he wants to charge me a foreigner fare. I don't have my Canadian passport with me."

Bharat started to laugh, "Why did you tell him you are a foreigner, you stupid ass?"

"He asked, so I gave him an honest answer."

The two junior controllers snickered at him, though they tried to hide it from Jag.

"Don't worry; I'll take care of that. Tell me how is life in Canada? Are you married? How many kids?" Bharat wanted to know all the juicy news.

"Bharat, I can't relax till I have the tickets. Please do this first and then I'll chat with you," Jag pleaded.

"You are not going anywhere in a hurry. See this fog? It will not lift till noon at least." Bharat gave him his professional opinion.

"I guess you still don't have the instrument landing system here, yet?" Jag asked the same professional way.

"Boss, we are not such a rich country as Canada yet." Bharat tried to be patriotic and defensive at the same time.

Jag came back to his tickets issue, "Why not get me my tickets first and then we'll talk."

"If you plan to stop in Lucknow and continue in the evening to Delhi, then you will have to pay a higher fare. Sometimes the flights are so late due to fog that they cancel the evening stop at Lucknow. Then you will waste your money." Bharat tried to counsel him about saving money.

"Bharat, it's very important for me to stop in Lucknow and then continue in the evening. It's a must. I don't care about the money. Please go and do it right now. Please."

Bharat noticed his old friend's impatience and got up from his chair. Jag handed him his wallet. "Do I have to come with you?"

"No, just enjoy your tea. I'll be back in a few minutes." Bharat answered him, confidently grabbing Jag's fat wallet full of Indian rupees and his Canadian credit cards. "If I am not back in 10 minutes, assume that I have run away with your wallet," Bharat kidded with Jag.

Jag could not sit still. He got up and started to walk around, trying to find the runway through the fog. He could not even locate the windsock to see if there was any wind blowing outside. It would have been the first indication if the fog might lift soon or not. There was no sign of the sun either. He glanced over to the wind-meter at one of the controller's tables; the needle was hiding below the zero mark. Jag felt frustrated; why did this have to happen today?

The peon showed up with four cups of Indian Chai tea and some biscuits. Jag knew he had to drink it whether he liked it or not as a sign of respect for Bharat's hospitality. The peon put a cup in front of him, put some biscuits on the plate, by the side of the cup, then he served the other two controllers.

Instead of drinking the tea, Jag played with the biscuits. He nibbled on them as if he were chewing on his thoughts. What if the fog did not lift till late afternoon? Then he might have to go to Delhi directly and give Lucknow a miss. He looked toward the runway: just a white wall of fog hung there.

"The wind seems to be picking up. I see some movement on the wind meter needle," one of the controllers said, breaking Jag's thoughts. Jag got up from his chair to see the wind meter. The needle was still below the zero mark. False hopes, he thought.

"From your experience, when do you think this fog will lift?" Jag asked the controller.

The other controller, who perhaps was his senior, felt he should answer, "It should burn by 10 AM." He shook his head from side to side to give his answer certainty. In India people are very sure about God and Nature. They speak with confidence. As a child, Jag had seen people betting on rain: when it was going to rain, what direction, what speed and how long. This, in a country which has several monsoon seasons!

Jag looked at his watch. It was only 8:30 AM. He felt relieved that he might make it to Lucknow after all! He might find Francis!

Just then Bharat walked up smiling and waving two airline tickets.

"See I got you them even for the Indian price and saved you 30%," he bragged and threw the tickets near Jag's tea cup.

"Thank you."

"Thank you for what? What are friends for? This was a piece of cake!" Bharat patted on Jag's back and continued, "Come on let's go to the flying club and have breakfast there. Boys will be very happy to see you after such a long time, and to see how well one of us has done!"

Jag remembered that in the old training days, everyone called the waiters, 'boys' even though most of them were around sixty years old. Jag was a favourite of most of the waiters, as he did not call them boys, but by their proper names to show respect. He used to think Bihari men were a bit rude and arrogant to people who were poorer than them.

"I'll buy the breakfast," Jag suggested, wanting to thank him for securing his ticket.

Jag got a dirty look from Bharat. "So if I visit Canada that means I have to buy my own food?" Then he hit Jag hard on his back to remind him of his Indian manners. Jag smiled meekly and followed him.

Jag looked at the other two controllers and asked them, "Can we bring something for you?" This was his adopted Canadian mannerisms. Both men shook their heads from side to side, meaning 'no thank you.' Their politeness for such words as 'thank you for asking,' showed in their eyes. Jag thought that they talked too much in the West, while here a simple nod or shake of the head said everything. Sometimes silence carried more meaning than so many words.

54

"Capt. N.N. Singh is doing your flight, so you can fly on the jump seat and get all the gossip of batch-mates in Calcutta. I hope you remember N.N." Jag nodded, following Bharat from the terminal building to his old flying club building.

Jag remembered N.N. Everybody called him N.N. His first name was so long that no body used it. N.N. had joined the flying club six months after Jag. He was the most humble Bihari Jag had ever met. N.N. was very meek and mild and called everybody *Bhaiya* - the big brother. This was a respectable way to address people in Bihar. Jag liked his meekness and helped him in his studies to catch up in the class and, for this, N.N. respected Jag. He had not seen N.N. since they graduated and all went their different ways.

Bharat continued, "I'll radio N.N. once they take off from Dum-Dum airport and let him know you will be on his flight. He will be so delighted. He always used to talk about you after you left. We all thought you would invite some of us to Canada, but you never wrote."

"I did answer a couple of people," Jag tried to remember the names he answered, but nothing came to his mind at that moment.

Bharat took him around like a prized trophy to reacquaint him with everybody. This old nostalgia bothered Jag; his mind was somewhere else. Boys came and saluted him and he tipped all of them well. The breakfast was good, like the good old days, but Jag could not eat. Perhaps too much milk or butter in the scrambled eggs.

His eyes kept wandering to the runway. The controller was right about his forecast on the fog. The wind picked up around 9 AM. Jag wanted to head back to find out about the flight. When they got back to the control tower at 9:30 AM, the sun was peeking through the fog a little bit.

Bharat got into his duty mode and, with a voice of authority, asked his assistants, "Has the flight taken off from Dum-Dum?"

"No sir, we haven't called it VFR - visuals conditions so far."

"Ah, make it VFR now. By the time they arrive here this fog will be burned off. Our friend Mr. Jag Mohan is in a hurry to go to Lucknow. He has to meet his girlfriend there. We can't delay him any longer." Bharat gave Jag a wink and a smile. This was the same wink they had shared all those years ago, when they talked about girls.

One of the controllers started on the telex machine while the other started to fill up the special weather form to make the airport for VFR conditions.

"Do your Canadian controllers give you such favors?" Bharat bragged.

"No, but then I fly by Instrument rules in such conditions." The answer flattened Bharat's ego. He did not have such a qualification and Jag felt just a bit remorseful for the reminder. The others all got back to their work in order to look busy and professional for their foreigner friend. Jag sat down and stayed out of their hair, he did not want his friend to feel inferior.

Bharat sat by the telex machine and slowly typed out a message and passed the holed strip through the machine. It made some noises and the strip went through. With a smile he turned to Jag and said, "I just sent a message to Capt. N.N. Singh that you are traveling on his flight, and would like to join him on the jump seat in the cockpit."

"Thank you." Jag was genuinely impressed.

"Mention not," came the quick reply with a nostalgic smile from Bharat.

In flying training days they used to talk like that amongst friends to impress each other with their knowledge of English. In those days people did not speak very good English in Bihar, and quite often trainee pilots used to make fun of the Chief Flight Instructor's spoken English by mimicking him. His English was the worst amongst the instructors. He would say something like this: "You come very early tomorrow morning and I'll start you night flying." Nobody understood why one had to come early in the morning to start night flying.

Jag remembered it and could not resist mimicking his old instructor's line loudly, and then both Bharat and he burst out laughing, to other controllers' surprise. Jag felt good sitting there, looking at the slow lifting of the fog and reminiscing about his old training days at this airport. For a few moments he forgot about Francis and relaxed.

One of the controllers announced very professionally, "Sir IA 404 has taken off from Dum Dum airport for Patna, Lucknow and Delhi. It's showing ETA here in 52 minutes."

"Good. See if you can contact Capt. Singh on Low Frequency. I want to talk to him." The official voice of Bharat re-appeared. After a while the controller was able to contact N.N. on the airplane radio. Bharat, who was monitoring his conversation, took the headset from the controller and spoke in the microphone.

Jag could hear only Bharat's voice: "Yes, yes the same Mr. J.M."

Jag smiled at his old pet name. They had a habit of calling each other by their initials.

Bharat continued on his headset, "Yes I'll personally bring him down."

He returned the headset to the controller and turned to Jag. "Capt. N.N. Singh wants to personally escort you on board his flight, so he has asked me to bring you down to the aircraft when he lands."

Jag smiled and bowed to Bharat to acknowledge thanks. "Hey Bharat, listen I am going to go down and walk around a bit. Ok?" Jag got up to go.

"Do you have any luggage to check in?"

Jag shook his head no, showing his small airbag in hand.

"Good, then I'll come down when the flight lands and walk you to the aircraft."

Jag nodded to his answer and headed down. For the first time since the morning Jag felt relaxed. He knew he would be able to meet Francis after all. If only for a few minutes.

He caught his reflection in a window and thought, 'God, how much weight I have gained in the last fifteen years! I wonder if Francis would even recognize me.' When he had left India he was a skinny, 135-pound twenty-four-year-old with a Dev Anand hairstyle. Now he was 40, bearded, long-haired and almost 185 pounds! Jag worried that he had become too ugly to see her again. He decided to head to the toilet to have better look.

In the mirror, Jag saw the face of a totally different man. Instead of a face of a dashing twenty-four-year-old, this was the face of a beaten-down, middle-aged, fat man. For a second the thought of canceling the whole idea became an option. He washed his face with the cold water and came out.

The building was getting crowded and he avoided going near the airlines' counter. He wandered around aimlessly to see if he could find a familiar face. He did not.

A few minutes later a public announcement came both in English and Hindi. Jag could not understand the heavily accented English announcement, but did make out the one in Hindi. The flight would be landing in about fifteen minutes. He walked to the glass window to see the runway. The fog had started to lift, the sun was peeking through, and the wind was blowing from the east. The pilot part of Jag thought about the difficulty Capt. N.N. could face landing with the sun in his face in this fog. He may not be able to see the runway till the last minute, or may abort his landing altogether. He kept his fingers crossed. Amazingly, as if God was personally hearing his thoughts, the fog lifted and Jag could see the runway from the terminal building.

The flight landed on time as it was announced. The aircraft, an old Fokker 27, had a bumpy landing. Bharat came down from the control tower and Jag walked to him. He had a big smile and commented, "Seems like N.N. was trying to teach his co-pilot how to land."

Jag smiled but did not answer.

"*Chalo*, lets go." Bharat tried to help Jag with his airbag. This is an Indian way to make one's guest feel welcome. But Jag resisted, answering him in Hindi. "*Theek hai.* It's ok. I can carry it."

Bharat headed for a side door leading to outside on the tarmac. The guard on the door saluted Bharat and let both of them go out. Only a couple of passengers de-planed. Capt. N.N. had come out and was doing his walk-around of the aircraft. Jag could see N.N. still looked the same, except a bit older.

He asked Bharat, "What about my ticket check-in?" Bharat grabbed it from him.

N.N. saw the two walking towards the aircraft and he came forwards for Jag and hugged him warmly. Then he looked at Jag's face and, pointing to his beard, asked, "What happened? Why such a sad looking face?"

Jag shrugged his shoulders.

Bharat handed N.N. Jag's airline ticket. "Sir, Capt. J.M. wants to check in."

They had a good laugh. All three old friends became like young trainee pilots at the same airport they started at twenty years earlier. Capt. N.N. waved at one of the airline uniformed staff, who came running.

"Capt. J.M will be traveling with me on the jump seat till Lucknow. Take the coupon out."

The airline staff obediently took the first coupon out without even glancing at Jag, then he politely returned the ticket to him. Jag was reminded of how power and hierarchy worked in India. How much he had forgotten in his time away.

N.N. became the Captain again. "Listen Bharat, we want to catch up some of the delayed time. So I will chat with you tomorrow on the return trip. Ok?" Bharat gave him the Indian nod.

Jag hugged Bharat and, before he could say thank you, Bharat read his mind and blurted out, "Mention not."

They shook hands very firmly and Jag followed N.N. inside the aircraft. No words were spoken. Emotions and sentiments were conveyed in that silence.

Once the aircraft leveled at the cruising altitude, Capt. N.N. took his headset off and his co-pilot became more attentive to the plane. The jump seat behind the two pilots' seat was a small pull-down seat. It was not comfortable to sit in, but Jag had done similar journeys several times in Canada. He could tolerate the discomfort for forty-five minutes.

N.N. turned and put his hand on Jag's hand, the way old friends do, then gave Jag a concerned look. "What's going on in your life my dear old friend, my *guru-ji*?"

"Before I tell you my life story, I need a big favour from you."

N.N. nodded, meaning to go ahead.

Jag continued with seriousness, "I need a car to pick me up from the tarmac at Lucknow airport and drive me to town and bring me back for the 4:30 flight for Delhi. It's very, very urgent. First, PLEASE do this, then we will talk about my life."

N.N. understood the urgency in Jag's voice. He put the headset on and contacted his airline's Lucknow ground office and ordered a car for Jag. Once confirmed, he took the headset off and turned to Jag.

"A car will pick you up at the tarmac and bring you back to the airport for the evening Delhi flight. Happy? Must be something very important in Lucknow for you to be rushing like this?"

Jag just nodded to his friend's query.

"Now what's going on in your life? Tell me." N.N. was very polite, although curious.

Jag thought for a few moments how to satisfy his friend's curiosity. The answer had to be short and precise to avoid having to provide any further details. Finally he spoke, "I am medically grounded from flying. I have been diagnosed with type two diabetes, so my aviation career has ended and I am in a mid-life crisis."

The answer was short with no drama and N.N. clearly understood Jag's dilemma but he could not come out with a verbal reaction. His face turned somber and sympathetic. It showed he really cared for his old classmate. With sincerity N.N. asked, "What do you plan to do now?"

"I'm not sure. I am trying to find answers. Maybe I'll go back to school and start a new career."

"At this age?" N.N. was not sure if he understood Jag right.

"Yes. People in Canada go to university even at the age of sixty to learn new things. I am only forty. I still have twenty-five years of working life left." With that, Jag gave a false smile of confidence to take away N.N.'s concerns. N.N. returned his smile but he had doubts about Jag's bravado. He felt he should stop probing his friend's life any further. Jag had told him more than enough in his short answer.

The plane's turbo-prop noise continued between two old friends' silence. Both understood that nothing could be talked about any further on the subject.

The airline car was waiting for Jag at the airport tarmac. Like a V.I.P. Jag rushed to it and ordered *"Chalo*, let's go."

Once the car was out on the highway to the city, he told the driver the address of the school where Francis taught. The driver in his white airline uniform and a funny cap kept nodding - yes, yes - to Jag while keeping eye contact with him through the rear mirror.

After Jag finished explaining to him, he spoke very politely, "Sir, there is no road to the school."

Jag understood his Hindi, but did not understand what he meant. "What do you mean by 'no road to the school?'"

"There is no road - only a mud narrow road from the highway. The car can't go. You have to walk or take a rickshaw."

Now Jag understood, "How far is the school from the highway?"

"Around half a kilometre." The driver apologetically answered as if it was his fault that there was no road to the school.

Jag looked outside the window. It was bright and sunny and getting quite hot, and then he answered the driver, "Fine, I'll take a rickshaw."

The driver continued in his polite Hindi, "Sir if you want to catch the evening flight to Delhi then you must come back to the corner latest by 3:45 sharp, or I have to leave…" He did not finish the sentence meaning 'Leave, without you.' It would have been inappropriate to threaten a V.I.P. with such words. But he did say the words latest and sharp in English to emphasize the urgency of his job.

Jag had to assure him. He knew his lateness may cause the driver problems with his Station Manager. "Not to worry, if I am not there by 3:45 PM sharp, you can go without me."

It did not take long for the car driver to arrive at the corner of the narrow dirt road. There were a lot of rickshaws parked there. They were used to taking students and others back and forth to the school. When Jag jumped out of the airline car, a lot of rickshaw drivers looked to him for a rich fare. Jag did not ask or bargained for the fare with the first rickshaw driver in the line. He just sat on the seat and ordered him, "School *chalo.*"

The rickshaw moved slowly on the dirt road and Jag felt the heat of the sun bearing down on him and the thumping of his heart inside his chest. His eagerness was oozing out of his face with beads of sweat.

The rickshaw arrived near the gate of the school. It was deserted. He looked at the rickshaw driver to seek any clues. The driver gave him a short answer, "Exams are going on."

"*Matlab* - meaning?" Jag asked him in Hindi.

"Kids finish school early." Another short answer.

"O.K. I want you to wait for me here, I have to go back to the highway. Don't worry about the fare. I'll pay you enough."

The rickshaw driver understood him and started to pull the top so he could have a short nap in the shade, while Jag headed for the old colonial-looking school building.

The building was empty. He walked in the hallway from classroom to classroom, looking for any sign of life. Finally, at the end of the hall, he saw a man sitting on a teacher's chair marking student exam papers. He knocked on the door and the teacher looked at him.

"*Ji?* - Yes?" The teacher asked a one-word question.

Jag answered in a hurry in English to emphasize the importance of disturbing him, "I am visiting from Canada and trying to find an old friend, Francis Wheeler, who teaches here and lives in teachers' quarters somewhere nearby. Can you help me to find her?" He made his last sentence a little more polite. But the word Canada had done the trick.

The teacher got up and, instead of shaking hands with Jag, said "*Namaste—ji*" the Indian version of hello. "You see we have exams happening, all the students and staff normally leave by 1 PM. I know Francis but I don't know where she lives." The teacher spoke in the halting English with difficulty.

Jag switched to Hindi to make him comfortable in his own language, "Do you think anybody around might know?"

Hearing Jag speak good Hindi, the teacher relaxed with this foreigner Indian and walked out in the hallway to see if he could find somebody who could help.

In the school playfield they saw a peon in khaki clothes walking away to the outside gate. The teacher shouted loudly,

"*Arre*'!" and when the peon turned to his shout, he continued at the same volume in Lucknow Hindi, "*Edhar aao* - come here."

The peon unwillingly turned and came towards them. He saluted the teacher and gave a quick glance to Jag.

"Do you know where Francis Wheeler madam's quarters are?"

The peon nodded to the teachers' question and turned to some blocks of two-story housing quarters on the other side of the playfield. Pointing to those quarters he gave a one-word answer.

"There."

Jag impatiently jumped in, "Do you know the quarter number?"

The peon shook his head NO and then answered Jag, "I don't know the number but I know her house."

"Can you take me there?"

The peon did not want to waste any more of his off time with this stranger in this heat. The teacher sensed it and immediately used his authority and ordered him, "The sahib has come from Canada, it's very urgent, so you take him and show him Francis madam's house. Understood?"

The peon unwillingly nodded YES this time.

Jag turned to the teacher and, in a very polite way, said, "*Namaste*, and thank you very-very much." Then he followed the peon who seemed in a hurry. Jag stepped back a couple feet from the peon and took out twenty rupees from his wallet and then moved up to the peon. He slipped twenty rupees in the peon's shirt pocket, and added, "Just for *chai-pani* - for tea."

The peon accepted the money with some false reluctance and smiled. Jag felt that he had made a friend who would not run away on him. Francis's quarter was not very far, but the sun was very hot and Jag started to sweat by the time they reached the second-floor quarters of Francis's building. Seeing a small varnish-coloured nameplate on the door with *Francis Wheeler D'souza* written on made Jag happy. Jag realized that she was married and that perhaps this might be her husband's surname.

'Finally I will see her,' thought Jag as he rang the doorbell. The wait was unbearable. Then the door opened with a certain quietness. It was not Francis but her old aunty-from-hell who had always disliked Jag. But she did not recognize him now. She just eyed the burly, bearded man before her with suspicion.

Jag noticed the fear of the unknown in her eyes and immediately blurted out, "I am a very old friend of Francis from a long time ago, is she home?"

This relaxed her. "No, she has not come home; she is still at the school."

"I just came from the school, and she is not there."

"Did you look in the library? Sometimes she sits there and marks exam papers before coming home."

"Ok, I'll go back and look again." Jag felt he should leave before she recognized him.

When he turned, Jag found that the peon had already left. He was on his own! He came out of the building and stood under a tree to wipe his sweat off his face as he checked his watch. He had very little time left before he needed to head back to the highway. He panicked that he'd miss his ride back to the airport.

Should he go back and try to find Francis in that big huge empty school building or head back to the highway? He wiped his face one more time with his now wet handkerchief and headed for the school building. He said to himself, "I am going to run up and down the whole building one more time and if I don't find her then I will head for the highway. So be it."

With that do-or-die determination he headed for the school building one more time. The sun was very hot and Jag did not have sunglasses. Even his eyes were burning. But just when he emerged from the tree's shade he saw a lone figure in a light blue sari, flat leather sandals and dark sunglasses coming through the school's play-field.

Jag's heart almost stopped. It was Francis. She looked exactly the same as he remembered her, except that she had a thin streak of grey hair, like Indira Gandhi, in the middle. Jag walked very quickly, straight towards her, blocking her path. She looked at him through her sunglasses while Jag waited to see if she recognized him. Finally, after a few moments, which for Jag was an eternity, she took her sunglasses off and said, "God, how come you have become so fat?" The familiar naughty smile showed up on her face. Jag was speechless; he did not know how to respond.

She put her arm in Jag's arm and turned him around to take him towards her quarter. Jag looked at his watch and panicked.

"Look Francis, I have only seven or eight minutes. An airline car is picking me up for the afternoon flight to Delhi. It's very urgent for me to be on it."

As if Francis did not hear him, she continued dragging him towards her quarters, and Jag felt he had no strength to stop her.

"You have to come see my daughter, and meet my husband in the evening. He knows you. I have told him everything about you." She gave him a confident look.

"But Aunty is at home. I just was there." Jag tried to stop her.

"Don't worry about Aunty. She is old now. What is your hurry?"

"Monica, my number two sister's daughter, is getting engaged this evening in Delhi. And my sister told me that if I did not make it then she'd never talk to me ever again."

"Ok. Come up at least to see my daughter and have a cup of tea. Then you can leave." Francis gave him an agreeable glance. Suddenly Jag felt he should have agreed to stay for a day at least. He wanted to be with Francis for a longer time. But now it was too late. He followed her to the quarters.

Francis opened the door with her own key without making any noise. Pointing to the sofa, she indicated that he should sit while she headed for the bedroom. She came back with a small sleeping baby and put her in Jag's lap.

"Her name is Monica too. Now, you look after her while I make some tea for you."

"Francis, please don't. I don't have time, I must leave soon."

Francis was already in the kitchen, "I am not going to let you go without having a cup of tea, first time in my house after so many years." She had already started the gas burner and put the water on to boil. After that she came to the kitchen door to see how Jag was doing with the baby.

"Seems you have had good practice looking after children. How many do you have?"

"I never married."

For the first time Francis gave Jag a concerned look.

"Why?"

Jag just shrugged and Francis felt that perhaps she should not pry into his life after such a long time. She quickly smiled and followed in jest, "Why no *gori*? Why no white girl picked you?" She heard the water boiling and turned back to the kitchen.

"Yeah, no girl proposed to me." Jag continued with her in jest. "Francis, please make the tea black - no sugar or milk."

Aunty sat beside Jag and spoke for the first time, "How can you drink black tea, no milk or even sugar?"

Jag felt Francis was listening to everything in the kitchen. He answered her softly, "I am diabetic. I can't have sugar."

Perhaps Aunty understood his answer because she nodded, as though understanding the reason for his sacrifice.

Francis brought him a black tea and put it on the table. She took the baby from him and gave her to Aunty. All this time the baby never cried or woke up.

"Are you still allowed to fly with Diabetes?"

Jag guessed that Francis heard him in the kitchen. He shook his head in no, then poured his tea in the saucer to cool it off faster. Jag blew on the tea and started to sip. He was afraid he might burn his tongue. Finally he just gulped it and stood up, in a hurry to run away from the past.

Francis noted his anxious desire to leave. She stood up with him and addressed Aunty, "I am going to walk Jag to his rickshaw and come back. Ok?"

Jag walked towards the door and nodded to Aunty. He was afraid of any more questions from her. He just wanted to leave as quickly as possible.

Francis and Jag walked together in the sun, side by side, towards the rickshaw. They were wordless, as if everything was already said and done. The rickshaw driver saw them coming and jumped out to let Jag sit. Jag climbed in and looked at Francis. She seemed calm, while Jag was struggling to control his emotions.

She touched at his elbow in a comforting way and said, "I am fine, you take care of yourself now. Bye."

Jag did not respond. He could not. The rickshaw started to move. Jag remembered the first time when he had dropped off

Francis at her Teachers' Hostel and waited by the gate hoping she would turn and wave at him; she never did. He felt he should turn and wave at her. But he could not. He was still trying to control his tears from rolling down his cheeks.

In Delhi, Jag rang the doorbell of his Number Two sister's flat. She opened the door and gave him a big laugh and hug. Then she barked at him, "So did you find a cure for your American disease?"

Jag smiled, nodded to her, and walked in.

SHAH JAHAN OF TORONTO

Rohit dipped his rag into the can, withdrawing wax, and slowly started to apply it on the front hood of the Jefferson Green 1947 Hudson Hornet. Why would they call the paint of a car Jefferson Green, he wondered? The spotlight and the sun-visor on the car looked strange to him. The whole car looked as if somebody had put a big bath tub upside-down and added some wheels as an after-thought.

The sweat pouring from Rohit's dark brown forehead and chest was a visual indication of how hot the day was. Wasn't this normally a cold suburb of Toronto? But the loud radio, a rock-n'-roll station told him it was thirty-three degrees Celsius outside and with the high humidity, the humidex made it feel like forty-two degrees.

In the morning, when Rohit's father, had dropped him off outside the shop, he had warned the naïve young man, "Rohit, it's going to be a hot day. Try to stay inside and drink lots of water, and be careful of the *loo*."

"What's *loo*?" Rohit had asked, opening the car door to get out.

To Rohit, his father had seemed transported in history. "My mother used to warn me too. 'Loo' is the dry hot-hot wind that blows in the summer. It sucks your body dry, and you die of dehydration. But that was in India. Here in Canada, it doesn't get so hot and dry."

Rohit, closing the car door, assured his father, "Don't worry, I'll be working inside all day."

After polishing this spaceship-looking 1947 Hudson for almost three hours, Rohit felt as if he had been hit by a 'loo.' He took his T-shirt off and started to rub the wax up and down.

His boss, David Jacobs, a short, thin man with lots of dots on his face told him he must polish the whole car by noon, because the owner of the Hudson, Mr. Frank Elkins, might be dropping by to have a look at it.

"Why would anybody restore such an old car and never drive it?" Rohit asked his boss.

"For their love affair." David smiled through a wide gap in his upper teeth as he continued, "Frank Spring designed this Hudson Hornet in 1947 with an expansive window to allow a spectacular view of the landscape. Back in those days, the cars were designed with aircraft themes. You see, peace and prosperity brought a new love affair with cars."

Opening the door of the Hudson, David invited him in. "Come sit inside to get a feel... Watch your sweat."

Once comfortably seated inside the cabin of the Hudson, it hadn't taken Rohit long before he could imagine himself transported into the fantasy world of Buck Rogers.

"And Jefferson Green?" the naïve man asked again, looking

over the hood of the car.

"I guess it was the name of the person painting the car at the time. Be very careful not to leave any marks of any kind anywhere on this car. Otherwise, Mr. Frank Elkins will kick your ass and mine." David handed him a can of wax, a lot of rags and then just walked toward the building, where, inside, there would be air conditioning.

"Yes, sir!" Rohit eagerly answered to his boss's back. His enthusiasm was that of a new employee. He was happy to have a weekend part-time job at $6.50 an hour at the Antique Car Restoration Shop and was beginning to acquire a new appreciation for old cars.

Rohit took a long breath and looked around. There was a grey 1952 Rolls. Next to it was a black 1953 Mercedes Benz, then a baby blue Ford Fairlane and next to it a 1955 pink Cadillac. The back of the Cadillac, with its double-winged fins, looked like an airplane. Still unsatisfied with David's answers, Rohit wondered why anybody would spend hundreds of thousands of dollars to restore these old cars and never drive them.

Rohit moved the rag rigorously up and down over the wax. Underneath, the green colour started to shine and reflect his face. He felt very proud of his work.

"You don't wax and rub up and down like that!" The old British-accented voice startled Rohit. Just then, some sweat dropped from his forehead on to the hood of the car. It was too late to hide it or to wipe it away.

Around eighty years old and almost six feet tall, Mr. Frank Elkins, dressed in a light yellow shirt, grey pants, thin matching tie and a white straw-hat saw where Rohit's sweat had dropped. To Rohit, he looked perfectly like a 'sahib,' just like the way

Rohit's mother had described the lavish British men from her childhood memories.

The 'sahib' took a clean rag from the box and gently wiped Rohit's sweat from the hood of the car and then slowly and smoothly rubbed the wax in a circular motion till the spot turned shiny.

"You first apply a thin layer of wax and then make a puff out of a clean rag and rub gently in a round and round motion. Like this." Pointing to the spot where he was rubbing the hood of the car, he continued, "See how easily it starts to shine."

Looking at the shiny spot Rohit meekly mumbled, "I'm new here. Nobody taught me how to shine this kind of car."

Mr. Frank Elkins, as if he did not hear what Rohit just said, took his hat off and gently put it on the front seat of the car. Then he undid his tie and rolled his shirt sleeves up carefully. He grabbed the can of wax and the rag and finally looked straight in his eyes, "Okay, I will teach you how to shine this kind of car. But first please shut that awful radio off."

Rohit shut the radio off and came back to the new silence around him. Rohit noticed all Mr. Elkin's actions were slow, not because he was old but because he was very precise. The British gentleman wiped the inside and outside of the wax can clean. He wrapped the rag around his first two fingers, put some wax on it and started to apply it on the hood very gently in a circular motion.

"It's like brushing your teeth with your fingers, slowly, gently in a rotating manner. Start to make the circle bigger and bigger and spread the wax very thinly." Mr. Frank Elkins looked up to see if Rohit was paying attention to his lessons. When he found him all ears, for the first time, he smiled at him.

"I'm sure you must have brushed your teeth with your finger some time?"

"No!"

"Have you ever seen your parents doing it?"

"No, I've a separate bathroom."

"My dear son, you're Indian, aren't you?"

Rohit could not understand the relationship between brushing his teeth with his finger, polishing an antique car, and his Indian heritage. But he remained polite in his answer to the 'sahib.'

"My grandparents moved to Trinidad and my parents moved to Toronto before I was born. I grew up here," Rohit felt it would be alright to update this old British man to the present day reality of Canada. "I consider myself a South-Asian Canadian."

"The new hyphenated Canadian?" There was no sarcasm, just curiosity in the old British accented voice.

"Yes!"

Mr. Frank Elkins took another rag, made a round puff of it, and started to polish where he had just put wax on the hood. "Have you ever seen your mother put on make-up?"

Without waiting for an answer from the young man, he continued, "Waxing and polishing a car like this is the same as putting on make up patiently, gently and carefully."

Rohit thought the old man was receiving some kind of sensuous pleasure from rubbing the car. The Brit smiled at the young man again.

Eager to start, Rohit picked up another rag and asked, "Should I start on the other side?"

"Certainly, my dear chap, I suppose that's what you are paid for, isn't it?"

Rohit rolled the rag on his first two fingers and dipped them in the can of wax, while Mr. Frank Elkins watched him with an examiner's look. Satisfied that the lad was attentive and quick to learn, he relaxed.

Rohit gently started to wax and rub the hood of the car the way Mr. Frank Elkins had just shown him. Realizing that the old man seemed to be happy with his work, he dared his curiosity again.

"It must cost a lot to restore an old car like this?"

"Yes." The Englishman maintained his upperclassman-ship.

"Why in the world would anybody spend thousands of dollars in restoring these old cars?"

"I suppose you've never been to India, have you?"

Rohit did not understand what the cost of restoring the car had to do with him not ever having gone to India.

Perplexed, he answered and questioned in the same sentence, "No, have you ever been to India?"

"Yes, I lived there during WWII."

"Social studies is not my strong subject, but what is WWII?" Rohit felt embarrassed. Now it was the old man's turn to be surprised at the ignorance of the young man.

"Don't tell me they haven't taught you about World War II in your school?"

"Oh, that," Rohit tried to hide his foolishness. "Yes, I know about World War II. It's just that I didn't understand when you said WWII. It happened in Germany. Right? I saw 'Schindler's List' last year. Is that the war you're talking about?"

"Schindler's List?" The old Englishman sounded surprised.

"Yeah, the Steven Spielberg movie! It won the Best Picture Oscar. It was about the Nazi army sending a whole bunch of

Jews to concentration camps during the Second World War. Right?"

Mr. Frank Elkins took a clean handkerchief out of his pocket and lightly wiped the sweat off his forehead. He thought the kid at least knew a little about WWII, not all was wasted. However, he was in no mood to discuss the quality of education in present day society at this time.

"Yes, that war. I was stationed in India - in Calcutta."

"I thought that war was in Germany, what were you doing in India?" Rohit thought he was asking a legitimate question.

Mr. Frank Elkins, a very patient man, finally felt a little annoyed with this young man's ignorance. "Don't they teach you any history in school?"

Although Rohit was not polishing at the moment, his whole brown body was still dripping with sweat. He made sure he did not drip any sweat on the car again. Wiping his chest with the T-shirt, he answered in a very unconcerned tone, "I don't like history."

Mr. Frank Elkins could not make up his mind whether he should teach this kid how to polish the car or talk to him about history. He just stared at him for a few moments and thought: the kid is not dumb; he is just not well-informed. But he was not in a mood to tell him the whole history of WWII. He made a shortcut and went on to the next chapter.

"I used to fly from Calcutta to Rangoon and then on to Singapore during the Second World War."

Suddenly, the young hyphenated South-Asian-Canadian's interest perked up. "You used to fly? You're a pilot? I've always wanted to fly a plane! So... you were a pilot!"

"Yes and no."

Looking at the confused face of Rohit after his answer, Mr. Frank Elkins thought he had better clarify his reply for this young man.

"I was a pilot with the Royal Air Force in India, but I don't fly anymore."

"Did you fly fighter planes or bombers?" Rohit was still eager and curious.

"Oh, I was merely a transport pilot. I flew Dakotas - DC-3's. It was just an old work horse of an aircraft. I mostly flew supplies." Mr. Frank Elkins felt that the kid wanted to think of him as some kind of a fighter or bomber pilot - maybe a war hero. For a moment the old man felt like lying about his own history to impress the kid, just to give him what he wanted to hear, but he didn't. Instead, he chose to change the topic, "Are you going to polish this car or gossip all day?"

Coming back to reality, Rohit immediately started to rub the hood of the car in a circular motion, while the old man watched him.

Mr. Frank Elkins' eighty-year-old body was still in good shape. He hardly sweated. The young man, on the other hand was sweating furiously. Despite his father's warning, 'not to yak away the whole day at work,' Rohit couldn't keep it to himself for long.

"Why would you spend so much money to restore such an old car?"

His repeated question took the old man down memory lane. "Oh, I forgot! You've never been to India."

"I don't see the connection between my question and your answer. What has my never having been to India got to do with this car?"

Now Mr. Frank Elkins felt it was necessary to tell this young man something about history. "I suppose you have never seen the Taj Mahal in your life, now, have you?" He paused for the answer.

Rohit barely shook his head 'no.'

"I'm sorry, I forgot. You told me you don't like history," the old man teased.

"And I've never been to India either."

Mr. Frank Elkins laughed as he nodded his head, remembering Rohit's other reminder.

"Let's take a quick lunch break and then continue with the polishing of the old bird. What do you say to that?" He looked at the car very fondly when he referred to it as 'the old bird.'

"Fine with me, you're the boss."

Sitting underneath a ceiling fan in the lunchroom at the back of the shop, the old teacher continued with the history lesson for his new student. "Did you know that Taj Mahal was the name of a woman?"

Shaking his head, more in disbelief than in surprise, the student answered, "All I know is it's one of the wonders of the world, and it's very pretty."

"Yes, you may not believe this, but it's true; Taj Mahal was the name of a woman." The British man spoke slowly, methodically, and with great passion. "The memorial was built in the sixteenth century by the great fifth Mogul emperor Shah Jahan of India. He affectionately called his favourite wife Mumtaj Mahal, meaning 'The Jewel of the Palace' - in short Taj Mahal. Shah Jahan loved his wife very much. I guess more than Romeo loved Juliet. Even after giving birth to thirteen children, Taj was still Shah Jahan's most beloved wife. Suddenly, enduring her

79

fourteenth pregnancy she fell ill. Shah Jahan forgot about ruling the country. He sat all day with her, but the doctors gave up on her. Before she died, Shah Jahan promised his wife that he was going to build a *Mahal,* a mausoleum, in her memory. It would be so beautiful that people from all over the world would come to see it and remember her as they marvelled over its architecture. It would stand forever as a reminder of her beauty and his love for her. The world would never forget the name of Mumtaj Mahal. She, and his love for her, would be immortalized. So, the great emperor Shah Jahan brought the best people from all over the world to build this Mahal. He imported jewels, diamonds and onyx from Iraq, Iran, Russia and Europe. Over a thousand elephants were used to carry the marble from Makarana in Rajasthan. It took twenty thousand people eleven years of excessive labour, cost and extraordinary diligence to finish the memorial. By today's standard, the cost of building the Taj Mahal is incalculable. It seemed the whole eclectic and adventurous Mogul dynasty came together in time and space to build this most romantic symbol of human love," the Englishman paused for a long breath. He closed his eyes, as if lost in a memory that wasn't his.

With a little saddened tone he continued again. "When it was finished, it was the most beautiful building of the time. Shah Jahan named it Taj Mahal. He wanted to build a black marbled tomb for himself on the opposite bank of the Yamuna River, and link the two by a bridge that would symbolize a love that transcended the flow of time itself. The dream never materialized. Shah Jahan was sad that his beloved wife died before the masterpiece of Mogul art was built, but was happy that the whole world would see it and remember her and his love and passion for her."

Rohit was amazed with the story. "How sad! She did not live to see it."

But the old man was more philosophical. "*C'est la vie* - that's life!"

"Did you see the Taj Mahal?" the curious lad asked again.

"Of course! After the war I invited my girlfriend to visit India. I took her to see it on a full moon night in October. The reflection of the white marbled Taj Mahal in the Yamuna River looked as if somebody had brought heaven to Earth. There I proposed to my girlfriend. There I asked Kathleen to marry me."

"And did she?"

The old nostalgic, romantic Englishman got up and started to roll his shirt sleeves down. His eyes were full of old memories. There was still a lot of passion in those eyes.

"She is still my wife. That old bird was the first car we bought here in Canada before we drove on our honeymoon." After a short pause of silence, he continued, "I'd love to surprise her one more time - take her for a ride."

Rohit followed the old man to the car. He picked up his hat from the front seat of the car and winked at him. "Do you think you'd have my Taj Mahal all polished up by next weekend, young chap?"

"Certainly Sir!" Rohit tried to mimic the British accent.

"Good, cheerio then! I'll see you next weekend and maybe I'll take her out for a spin." With that, the old man put on his hat and left.

During the week, Rohit found books on the Taj Mahal and post-war antique automobiles in the school library. He did not want to go to his weekend job unprepared for his next history lesson.

As soon as he arrived at the Antique Car Restoration Shop, and before he even got a chance to say good morning to his boss David, he found a clean rag and started to dust 'the old bird.' He had brought his books from the library to show them to Mr. Frank Elkins. He was very proud of his research and information on the Taj Mahal and the car.

He cleaned the floor as David had asked him to do. He cleaned the back room. He polished another car with the same attentiveness he had learned from the Englishman the weekend before. At every small noise he looked at the door, hoping to see Mr. Frank Elkins walking in. The day went by and the old Brit did not show up.

At the end of the day, Rohit thought maybe Mr. Frank Elkins would come in the following weekend. He renewed the books at the school library for another week. He re-read some of the pages and looked at all the pictures in the books. By now, he had memorized the size and dimension of the Taj Mahal. He also wanted to remind Mr. Frank Elkins that the diamond Kohinoor, in the crown of Queen Elizabeth II, was taken from the Taj Mahal, and so many other stories, probably the old man had forgotten.

The whole next Saturday passed by. Rohit kept on looking at the door. Finally, late in the afternoon, he could not control his curiosity and walked into David's office.

"I thought Mr. Frank Elkins was going to take his car for a drive. What happened?"

David looked at him soberly. "Sad news, Rohit, Mrs. Kathleen Elkins passed away last weekend. Probably the old man won't be coming for a few weeks."

Rohit was dumbfounded. Something inside him wanted to say, "*C'est la vie* – that's life!" But instead he walked out mumbling to himself, "Mumtaj died before the Taj Mahal was completed."

PROPWASH

Jag Mohan had been in Canada for almost five years. He had overcome his nervousness of being a new immigrant and, although he still talked with an Indian accent, people no longer looked at his face and said, 'pardon me,' because they did not understand him.

Jag noticed that his boss, Frank, still had his British accent even after living in Canada for over twenty-five years. He felt he could continue with his accent as long as he spoke slowly and used local slang. He started to mimic some of his students' and colleagues' spoken style and words. He particularly liked the accent of one of his Quebec students. He loved speaking in his Indian-Quebec-accented English. People laughed at Jag's mimicry, but he did not mind being made fun of because he also made fun of himself.

Lack of any ego earned a lot respect for Jag from his friends. Frank, who had flown Dakotas from Calcutta to Rangoon during WWII, started to invite him either for lunch at a nearby Legion club on Friday afternoons or for a beer before heading home in the evenings. Frank was very open with Jag about the business and its trends.

The flying training slowed down in winter in Edmonton. Jag learned buzz words like downturns and layoffs. Bankruptcies. His own salary was based on the number of hours he flew in a month, and winter months were hard on his pay slips. Their flying school was the smallest in Edmonton and was not well financed. Jag started to understand that Frank was a good man but not an astute businessman and so, during one of these Friday afternoon beer sessions, Jag thought of running an idea with Frank to improve the business.

After putting half a beer in his stomach, Jag developed enough courage to speak about it. "Mr. Elkins," Jag still called Frank by his last name; he had not become Canadian enough to call him Frank yet. "Why not we go to people and teach them flying, instead waiting for them to come to us?"

"Jag, are you switching into Hindilish again after half a beer?" Frank understood Jag's English, but sometimes he did not understand Jag's thoughts, at least not the way Jag expressed them. Jag knew his weakness; his mind still might be thinking in Hindi while he spoke in English. This translation of thoughts did not always come across properly. Jag realized he had to master to speak his thoughts in proper Canadian English.

Jag tried again, this time more slowly, "What I mean is, we go to small towns and run satellite flight schools in winters, while we are slow here in Edmonton. Alberta is booming and the oil is paying big salaries to people in small remote towns. Perhaps they may take interest in flying lessons. We can't compete with the big schools here, so we go to the people in small towns and teach them there, in their own towns."

"We tried running a satellite school four years ago, but it did not work, and we lost money. There were not enough students and then some dropped off in the middle." Frank spoke from experience.

Jag did not feel discouraged, "Yes, but then the economy was not as strong as it is now. People are making a lot more money working in the oil patch. I have two students who drive seventy miles on the weekend to take flying lessons here. They tell me that a lot of their friends would love to take flying lessons, but driving every weekend on icy roads stops them. Why not, we go and teach them locally?"

"You want another one?" Pointing to his empty beer glass, Frank asked. Though Jag very seldom had two beers on the same evening, he nodded. He needed a 'yes' from Frank on his idea. He felt confident that in time he could persuade his boss.

After Frank had a long sip from his second beer, he asked Jag, "You - a boy from hot and over populated Calcutta, want to go into the small towns of Alberta in the middle of winter, with minus thirty degree temperatures, so you can freeze your ass and teach flying there?"

By now the usual quota of Jag's first beer had already started to affect his brain. Without even thinking for a moment, he belched out a "yep."

"So, exactly how do you want to do this?"

Jag had not worked out an action plan - so far it was just an idea. He had to buy some time with Frank to work this out. He did not think Frank would agree so quickly and ask all the logistical questions.

"Let me talk to my students on the weekend and plan it all out. Then I can tell you on Monday, yeah?"

"Fair!" And with that Frank gulped down the rest of his second beer and got up. He always rushed his beer drinking and left in a hurry to get home to his wife, Kathleen. Jag used to sit and drink alone after he had left. Jag felt elated and enjoyed sipping his beer slowly, alone, while his brain started to figure out his future plans. This was his first turn to prove that he could do something on his own in Canada instead of just working for other people. He wanted some proof for himself that he was smart and enterprising, even when his spoken English was not at par.

Over the weekend, he discussed his plans with his two students from Whitecourt, a small northwestern town in Alberta which was rich with oil and gas drilling. Rudi, one of his students, suggested that he visit Whitecourt on the weekend and meet all the potential students in person. It would be more effective and he would have a chance to see the airport and town. Jag liked the idea, partly because he had never ventured to the small towns of Alberta.

When he talked to his colleagues at the flight school, they all laughed at him. One of them even warned him, "Those red neck cowboys in the oil patch will skin your brown ass alive."

Jag, who was not familiar with all the slang and swear words, ignored them. Frank, on the other hand, agreed to his idea very easily and even approved his one-night stay in a motel in Whitecourt.

Whitecourt airport was a small dirt strip at the top of a hill only a kilometer from the town. One of the oil company's twin otter planes flew in and out every day to pick and drop off crew from remote areas. It had a small shack as a waiting area. Though Whitecourt was small, it had all the necessary facilities and the

Alaska Highway ran right in the middle of the town. Because of gas and oil, the average wage was quite high. The town had earned the notoriety of being the second highest consumer of alcohol in the province that year.

Rudi picked Jag up from the little airport. He had booked him a room at the Blue Grass Motel right at the end of the runway strip. The motel was next to a Kentucky Fried Chicken, in a single-story, dirty, old building where roughnecks from the oil patch stayed. It was very basic, but Jag didn't care. He was on a quest and could only think of returning a conquering hero!

The meeting with potential students was set in the evening in the local high school. Rudi had run a little ad in the local paper called Whitecourt Star, known to the locals as 'The Rag.'

"I figure there should be about 20 students or so," Rudi estimated aloud.

The news was a sweet tune in Jag's ears. Frank had told him as long as there were ten students ready to start he would let him run the satellite school. Rudi dropped him off at the Blue Grass Motel with a promise to pick him up in a couple of hours. Jag sat in his small room with an excitement he could not control. Finally, he was going to be somebody in Canada! He would run his own satellite school, for which he would solely be responsible. He would prove to the world that he was no dummy. He could not rest. He made notes, over and over again. How was he going to do his speech? How was he going to do the questions and answers? He went over his notes three or four times, just to make sure he was well-prepared.

Rudi drove him to the school and, after a brief introduction, gave him the floor. For the first time Jag had a chance to see everybody's face. He felt nervous. He was the only brown face in the class and some of them seemed as though they had driven in straight from some mud-fields. All of them wore big muddy boots and faded work jeans. 'So these are the rednecks who are going to skin my brown ass,' Jag thought to himself. Then with a smile he spoke with his Indian accent, very slowly and very clearly.

The speech basically covered what would be involved in the private pilot license training, the costs and dates and times of the classes. Yes, he answered one mud-covered man, he would move to Whitecourt and live there during the three months of the satellite license period. As he summarized the information, he realized that his entire information session lasted less than ten minutes.

Jag waited for questions. There were none. He wondered if they had problems understanding his English. He looked at Rudi for help.

Rudi prodded them again. Finally one hand went up and an unassuming-looking, middle-aged man asked, "Do I get a discount if I pay you the full fees in advance?"

Jag finally felt relieved. A few people laughed loudly and some spoke to the middle-aged man, "Way to go John! Always thinking of saving a buck, eh?"

Jag learned his first, and most common, Canadian slang word, 'eh.'

"No, you can pay a five hundred dollars in advance and then pay as you go. I'll let you know when your five hundreds are up. No discounts." Jag felt encouraged.

"Well then let's go for a beer, if nobody has any questions," John said.

One by one, they walked out, each first leaving a cheque on the table in front of Jag. He looked at Rudi with surprise.

Rudi smiled and told him, "I told them on the phone that if they are serious then they had better bring their cheque-books with them."

Jag counted. There were sixteen cheques in front of him — all signed and dated. Jag could not control his smile.

In the pub that the locals nicknamed 'The Zoo,' none of his potential students let Jag buy his own beer. Almost all of them bought him a round. In the Blue Grass Motel Jag spent the rest of his night by the commode instead of in his bed. This was a good initiation for an Indian man in cowboy country.

Correction: This was a good initiation for an *East Indian* man in a redneck cowboy country. And Jag liked it. He felt he could fit in with these people like a glove. It gave him a new sense of confidence and cockiness. But Jag still needed to learn a few more tricks.

Setting up the satellite flight school in Whitecourt was quite easy. The Department of Transport gave the approval within one week and even appointed one of the local doctors to do all pilots' medical examinations. Jag was offered room and board, and one of his students offered him an old car to drive while he was there.

Jag was set and Frank was very happy with him. The office book-keeper gave him a crash course in keeping track of all the money. With his small suitcase, and flight training supplies packed in a Cessna-150, Jag headed for his new venture in Whitecourt.

Out of the first sixteen cheques Jag had received, two trainees had medical problems and had to drop out, but then three more students showed up the day he arrived to start the class. Jag was quite happy. He made up in his mind that he was going to be a good, hard-working instructor.

In the very first meeting with his students, Jag emphasized punctuality and discipline about attending the ground school. He had only three months' of license for the satellite school so they better not miss any class or appointment for their flight training. If they couldn't make it then they had better exchange that appointment with one of their classmates. He circulated everybody's phone numbers with the whole class, so all could work as a group.

The first problem Jag faced was the education level of his students. Some of his students were farmers and others were tradesman, like plumbers and welders, who were financially rich and spoke good English, but could not comprehend Navigation and Meteorology. Jag did not know that a lot of Canadians could make a great living as a farmer or tradesman without being able to read or write. He paired students who could read with those who had problems reading. It worked out well, but it slowed down the overall progress of the class.

On the phone, Frank was encouraging. He suggested sending up another aircraft and instructor on the weekends to help him in the flight training. That would free Jag up so that he could spend more times with slower students. Jag did not like the idea but he knew it was the only way to train all of his students in three short months.

Things started to move more smoothly. Jag was able to spend time socializing with his students. He picked up more slang. Watch-m-call. Horny, a word not synonymous with cars or bulls. And that 'John' wasn't always a man's name.

At the airport one day, a new student asked him, "Where's the John?"

"John is not flying today," Jag replied.

The student smiled and repeated his question, "No, I mean where is the loo?"

"There is no Lou in the class, is there?"

"I mean the toilet?"

"Ah, of course. Toilet." Jag pointed to a little shack.

"You mean that outhouse?"

"No it's not an outhouse, that's the toilet." Jag said with an emphasis.

And then one of his Texan students told him his experience with fishing over the weekend. His drawl sounded like different words to Jag. The student said he went for *ass-hole fishing.* Jag was surprised and asked, "What is ass-hole fishing?"

"No, no! Not ass-hole fishing. I am not gay. We go over ice on the lakes, when it's frozen, then drill a hole and fish there. It's called ice-hole fishing." The Texan drawl still confused Jag - ice sounded like ass to him

"Then why don't you say ice-fishing instead of ass-hole fishing?"

They both laughed at each other's accent. Jag's vocabulary of local sayings increased. He noticed people used word play to tease. He enjoyed the game.

The students were doing well in the class. Most of them were mechanically very adept and understood the technical side of flying. When some of the students started to fly solo Jag had more time to explore. He would go to the coffee shop downtown, next to The Zoo bar. They had a daily lunch special for $4.99 which included soup, a main course, a piece of pie and a very watery coffee. The locals knew who he was and, although he was the only east-Indian in town, they welcomed him.

He earned his respect and status. This gave Jag a new sense of confidence, bordering on cockiness.

His usual waitress, a tall, skinny blonde named Judy, was always friendly with him, chatting away as she took his order which was always the same, the lunch special. Jag thought that she liked him.

"Are you going take me flying?"

"You mean for a joyride?" Jag tried his new vocabulary of words with a smile.

"Is that what you call flying?" Judy smiled.

"Yeah, for those who want to go for a fun flight, it's called joyride or a fam flight."

"What's a fam flight?"

"It's for potential students who want to familiarize with flying before they commit to full lessons."

"Ah! Then I will just go for a joyride, if that's okay with you?" Judy's smile became flirtatious.

"And would you like to join the mile-high club at the same time?" Jag retuned her flirtatious smile with one of his own new cocky smile.

"And what's that?" Judy kept her smile and circled her lips in a sexy way.

"I'll tell you when I take you up for a joyride."

"And when will that be?"

"Soon."

"Hope it's sooner than later." With that Judy walked away, while Jag got lost in his imaginary dreams of how he'd introduce Judy to a mile-high club.

The next day Jag went for lunch earlier than his usual time. The coffee shop was not busy. But, instead of Judy, another waitress, a short chubby woman with 'Nona' written across her name tag, came to take his order.

"The same?" Nona opened her order book to write down his order.

"What happened to Judy today?"

"She's sick."

"I hope nothing is serious with her," Jag tried to sound casually concerned.

"Nah. You didn't give her anything serious." Nona leaned toward him and continued in whisper. "She's got one of those monthly, girly things. She always has problems with that."

Jag was not ready for such detailed personal information about Judy. Nona knew this new immigrant would be surprised with her blunt remarks and smiled as he blushed.

To change the subject Jag asked, "Can I see the menu?"

With a sense of 'you are putting me through some unnecessary work,' Nona went to get him a menu. The coffee shop was still empty so she stood next to him, clicking and tapping of her ball point pen while she waited to take his order.

Jag saw the sloppy hand-written note at the top of the menu for the daily special: Chicken noodle soup, Shepherd's pie with green peas, apple pie and coffee for $4.99. Jag ignored the note and tried to look at the menu. Nona knew he was killing time to let his embarrassment pass.

Then she surprised him with her next question, "I hear you are going take Judy up for a joyride and make her join the mile-high club. Is that so?"

"Who told you that? Judy?"

"We don't keep any secrets in this town. Just read 'A Little Birdie Told Me' in the weekly Rag and you'd know that about us."

"I suppose now you too want to join the mile-high club?" Jag shot back.

Nona burst out in a healthy chuckle, while her big breasts jumped up and down. She moved closer to his ear and whispered, "I'll join any club you want right here. You don't have go even that high. You just tell me when." Her chuckle shortened to a challenging wide smile.

Jag avoided an eye contact with her. "I think I'll have the special."

Nona jotted down "1-special" in her order book and, before she turned to go, she said, "Even your brown face turns to red when you blush. I like that, you look cute."

The next day Jag looked through the coffee shop window to see if Judy was working. Once he saw her, he entered the coffee shop and sat at his regular table.

Even before Judy put his customary glass of water on his table, Jag shouted, "So you are telling the whole town now that I am taking you for a joyride, eh?" He used "eh" first time in his life. He thought he sounded very local.

"I only told Nona." Judy defended herself.

"And you told her that I have asked you join the mile-high club?"

"I just asked her if she knew what a mile-high club was."

"I suppose now she is going put this in the 'A Little Birdie Told Me' in the Rag?"

"No, it's just between us. We are good friends." By now Judy was almost meek in her response.

Jag suddenly realized how harsh he was being. How uncomfortable and sorry Judy seemed.

"Sorry. Nona was pulling my leg yesterday." He smiled at Judy and broke the tension.

"Yeah she told me. Said you turned red," Judy smiled back. "I'd have loved to have seen that."

"Get out of here. Go get me my special." Jag was back to his normal self. He noticed Judy had lipstick and a bit of make up on her today. Her top had a lower cut and her small breasts were slightly visible through it. When she turned he saw her jeans were tight and her small, rounded bum looked VEEEEERY nice.

By now Jag had learned what the word horny meant. He felt happy at that moment. And horny.

Jag kept thinking about Judy throughout the afternoon. Whenever he tried to concentrate on something else, he remembered her smile, her voice, her bum in her jeans... He asked Boris, one of his housemates, if he knew her.

"Yeah, what about her? Do you want to lay her or what? She is a nice girl. She doesn't do those things."

"No, no such thing." Jag tried to be discreet. "She asked me to take her up for flying and I was wondering if that would be okay. Like this is a small town and I don't want people to misconstrue it, eh?"

Boris had a loud laugh. "You keep using those big English words and people are going to talk about you. And if your intentions are to get laid then I can introduce you to some other girls, who would be much easier to chase." He winked at Jag meaning *you-know-what-I-mean.*

"Thanks, I'll let you know."

Boris added, "Don't be shy about it, okay?"

After that advice from Boris, Jag decided not to take Judy flying. No mile-high club after all.

"Are you going to take me flying for real or you BS-ing me around?" Judy confronted him in the coffee shop. "Or was that all smart talk?"

"Do you know what joining the mile-high club even means?"

"Yeah, sort of!" Judy's lips circled. She had a dare-me look in her eyes.

"Are you ready to join then, eh?" Jag dared her back.

"Depends. Who's asking and when," Judy bent down to pick up the menu from his table and continued in whisper, "and if I am in the mood."

Jag felt hot, excited and nervous. He did not expect such a challenge from Judy. Instead of standing up to her challenge, he decided to play a trick on her, using his newfound play on words... "Alright, I'll take you flying this afternoon, what time do you get off?"

"Really? You are not pulling my leg or BS-ing me? Are you?"

Jag shook his head NO.

Judy continued very excitedly, "I get off at two."

"Okay, you pick up a gallon of prop wash from Maljo's and bring it to the airport. Tell Lorne to charge it to my account. Okay?"

"Okay!" Judy replied with great excitement in her voice.

Now prop wash is not a detergent used to wash the propeller of airplanes but rather the wind behind the propeller when it's running. Jag had been the brunt of so many word tricks played on him by the locals that now it was his chance to have a bit of fun. He called over to one of his students, Lorne who ran Malijo, the automotive shop and set up the rouse.

Judy arrived at his store promptly at 2:00 PM to pick up a gallon of prop wash. Lorne empathetically told her, "Gee Judy we just ran out of prop wash. I guess Jag is taking you up for a joyride, eh?"

Judy nodded, she was in a hurry. "Where else can I get it?"

"Check it at Texaco or Esso on the way to the airport. Do you want me to phone them?"

But Judy was out of the door and never heard the last part of Lorne's sentence.

Judy got the same answer as Lorne's at Esso and Texaco and then at Gulf and then at a couple of Independent automotive shops. She thought somebody was conspiring against her airplane ride. Then she bumped into Boris and asked him, "Hey Boris where can I get a gallon of prop wash? I have checked all over the town. Jag asked me to pick it for him and he is taking me for a plane ride."

Boris had a long loud laugh. The laugh gave Judy a clue that Jag was pulling her leg. Then Boris asked her, "Do you know what prop wash is? It's the wind behind the propeller when the engine is running. It's not a liquid detergent."

Judy felt angry and hurt. Two small teardrops rolled out of her eyes. She did not go to the airport. Jag did not dare to go the Coffee shop for a couple of days. Not until the following Wednesday when a blurb was printed in the 'A Little Birdie Told Me' column. "A Local waitress is looking for a gallon of prop wash for our flight instructor so she can go for a joyride. Can anybody help her to find it?"

When Jag read it he felt terrible and thought he owed Judy an apology. The coffee shop was almost full and his usual seat was taken. He took another table. He noticed quite a few copies of The Whitecourt Star were lying around.

Judy did not even look at him. She totally ignored him. Finally Nona came to him with no menu or glass of water and in her loud voice asked, "The usual, lunch special, eh?"

"Is Judy not going wait on me, eh?" Jag asked meekly.

"You're in the dog house, mister."

"What does that mean?" Jag became meeker.

"You're up shit's creek." Nona became louder.

"What kind creek is that?"

Nona felt Jag was pulling her leg now. She gave him a stern look. "What are you going to have? We are very busy today." She implied that he was wasting her time.

"Ok, I'll have the usual. The special."

Judy never came to Jag's table to wait on him after that and he stopped going to the coffee shop. He began making sandwiches at home.

The spring came early that year. Jag managed to finish his class early. Jag was proud of his achievement; each one of his students had graduated. Frank promised him a promotion and a raise when he returned to the head office in Edmonton. Although Jag looked forward to returning to Edmonton, he knew he would miss this small town with its assortment of eccentric but friendly people. Jag decided to stay for an extra week, if only to relax and have a look at the countryside.

One sunny and warm Sunday, Boris had pulled his small boat from the garage and was polishing it to get ready for the summer. Jag came out of the house and watched Boris and his friends working hard on preparing the boat for the coming season.

Jay Bajaj

After watching them for a few moments, Jag asked, "Hey Boris, I am going to town, do you want me to pick up anything for you guys, eh?"

"Nah. We are okay."

When Jag headed for his car on the street, Boris shouted back. "Just bring us some elbow grease, we are running out of it here. You can get it from Maljo."

"Okay." Jag drove away in his shiny new ford Mustang.

Lorne greeted Jag very warmly when he arrived at his automotive shop and asked, "Hey Lorne, Boris is polishing his boat, and wants me to pick up a pound of elbow grease."

Lorne smiled, "Gee Jag we just ran out of it."

"Where else I can get it?"

"Check at Texaco or Esso near the airport. Do you want me to phone them?"

"Nah, I am going that way, I'll check."

"Have a coffee first, Jag." Lorne suggested. Jag waved 'no' behind his head and left.

Jag got the same answer at Esso and then at Texaco. Then at Gulf and a couple of Independents. He did not suspect anything and continued searching for a pound of elbow grease.

Then he bumped into Dennis-the-welder, one of his graduate students, and asked him, "Hey Dennis, where can I get a pound of elbow grease, eh? I have checked all over the town! Boris asked me to pick it up for him. He is polishing his boat."

Dennis smiled; he was a gentleman and he politely explained to his east-Indian flight instructor, "Elbow grease is slang for helping out your friends when they are working on something. It's sharing the labour. Perhaps Boris is pulling your leg."

Jag laughed, realizing that it was a fair turn of events; after all, he had gotten away with a lot in this little town.

When Jag returned home Boris and his buddies were still polishing the boat. Jag gave them a false apology, "Sorry Boris, I forgot all about your elbow grease."

Boris and his buddies saw the white lie.

"Not to worry about it, we can manage," Boris said, putting a little extra effort into his polishing.

In the following week's Whitecourt Star, it printed a blurb in their 'A Little Birdie Told Me' column: *Our highly professional, smart flight instructor is looking for a pound of elbow grease so he can polish his buddie's boat. Can anybody help him to find it?*

Jag read the news and decided to go to the coffee shop for lunch. Judy walked to his table with the Rag. She had the Rag's page open and dropped it in front of him. Jag did not say anything, just looked at her with rabbit's eyes.

"I've a pound of elbow grease for you, if you want to buy it?"

"And how much it'd cost me?"

"A gallon of prop wash." Her circled lips turned in to a smirk. She picked up her newspaper and turned to walk away from him.

Jag whispered, "I am very sorry Judy."

She turned, smiled at him and then waved at Nona to wait on him.

EVERYTHING WILL BE FINE

"Mother expired."

Ken repeated the two words when he did not hear a response from Jag.

"I suppose it is sad news for you Jag, isn't it? I am sorry to have you woken up so early in the morning." Ken kept talking on the phone. "I just came on my shift and the night clerk did not know how to contact you. He told me about this telegram when I came in this morning. It came in last night from India. We don't get telegrams here in Canada. People usually phone."

Jag shifted in his bed. His voice was groggy, "Thanks Ken. Really appreciate it for phoning me so promptly." Jag's mind was still foggy; he couldn't quite grasp the gravity of the message.

"I am sorry to give you such bad news first-thing in the morning." Ken paused a moment but then his curiosity got the better of him. "Is that how they say it in India, 'expired,' when one passes away?"

Now Jag was wide awake and wanted to get off the phone as quickly as possible, "Yeah, it's a standard telegram code number for such messages, when you send one. You don't have to write the whole message on the form. The clerk decodes it and sends it by telex."

"I am very sorry about the news. Please let me know if I can do anything."

"Yeah, thanks a lot. Could you please print this whole telegram out for me? I will pick it up from your office a bit later. I may need it to book my airline ticket on compassionate grounds."

"Sure, sure."

"Thanks again Ken, I'll see you a little later." With that Jag quickly hung up the phone.

'Mother expired.' Jag sat up in his bed and said the words in his mind. He did not feel any sadness about it. He had been preparing himself for this news for some time now. He understood this would eventually happen and so no tears rolled from his eyes. Still, he was a bit surprised at his detachment.

Jag got out of the bed and headed for the bathroom to begin his daily preparation for the office. He had just moved a few months ago into the small town of Whitecourt where he had started as a working partner with a two small airplanes charter company. The business was booming and both partners were flying a lot. Jag was happy and was expecting a brighter future. He would have preferred that his mother passed away a bit later, when he was more successful.

Jag went through his shower analyzing how he should feel about the news. What sort of expression should he have on his face when he told his friends and colleagues the news? In his mind, or heart perhaps, he did not feel anything, but he could not show people his lack of feelings. The truth was that the distance from India had created an emotional distance from his family. Perhaps the definition of 'home' had blurred with the passage of time in Canada. This was his new home and his friends here were his new relatives. He had started to feel more at home in Canada than in India. What would he do there? How would he feel when he arrived back in India? Jag felt very uncertain in the bathroom. As a pilot, he felt his mind was flying in a thick fog and he had no instrument to follow. In aviation they called it being disoriented. He looked in the mirror to find any such signs on his face. He found two days' growth. 'I might as well not shave it, it suits a grim look.'

Jag really didn't want people to give him condolences. He wondered how he should go in and out of Ken's office without fussing about his grief, or lack of grief. He parked his car outside Ken's office and approached the door. He found an envelope stuck to the office door with his name on it. Perhaps Ken had gone for a coffee break.

Jag ripped the envelope open. The telex was printed on cheap recycled paper with some sort of dot-matrix printer. The ink had started to fade but it was still readable. There was a lot of technical mumbo-jumbo about the routing of the telex at the top of the paper, and then halfway through, Jag found the two words: Mother Expired, Kaka. It was sent by his younger brother who was called Kaka at home. He felt assured now that the news was accurate.

At the airport his partner, John, had already arrived. As usual, he was busy looking at some bills and invoices. Their receptionist was not yet in which relieved Jag. He would not have to go through another man-with-grief experience. He felt this whole process of expressing condolences by the people in the west a bit unreal, like saying 'sorry' when one did not really feel sorry. Jag had just learned another English word, 'lip service.'

Jag wanted the least amount of drama when he walked into John's office. John looked up and said, "Morning Jag."

Jag feebly answered, "Morning," and then put the printed telex in front of John. "My mother passed away last night, I just got the telex."

For a big guy, John was quite an emotional man. "Oh my God, I am very sorry, very sorry to hear this." He came around and immediately wrapped his muscular arms around Jag in a tight hug.

Jag did not feel comforted by the gesture. He carefully freed himself. John looked with genuine sadness at Jag, "Are you okay?"

Jag nodded with an expression of I-am-fine. "I'll need to go home for the funeral," he mumbled.

"Yes, definitely. How long do you want to go for?"

"Maybe two weeks."

"It's okay if you want to stay longer, I can manage here." John was generous.

"I'll phone you if I need to stay longer." Jag was ready to leave the office.

John pulled out a cheque book and hurriedly wrote him a cheque for two thousand dollars. "Here, some emergency funds, you never know when you'll need it. Right?"

Jag took the cheque and the telex copy from the table and then extended his hand to John. John warmly shook it.

"Thanks," nodded Jag and walked out quickly.

Once he was back in his car he felt satisfied with his first performance of the morning without much feeling of grief.

It was only in the Air Canada flight from Edmonton to Toronto that Jag looked at his Indian passport and panicked.

Expired. Like his mother. He was able to arrange his ticket from Edmonton-Toronto-New York with Air Canada and then to New Delhi and Calcutta with Air India and Indian Airlines. The local travel agent knew he was a pilot and assumed he must have all his travel documents up to date. Now, onboard the Air Canada flight Jag realized the uncertainty of his predicament. He had become a Canadian citizen only a month ago but hadn't yet applied for a Canadian Passport. He was told that once he became a Canadian citizen, he would have to give up his Indian citizenship because India does not allow dual citizenship. Now what to do?

"Think Jag think," Jag tried to calm himself. The flight was somewhere near Winnipeg. He still had about two hours before he would land in Toronto before catching his flight to New York. He figured he'd be landing in Toronto around 4:00 pm and the Indian consulate office might still be open. Perhaps they could give him a temporary extension on his passport. He pulled out his Canadian Pilot's license, his Indian passport and the "Mother Expired" telex - which he had highlighted with a yellow marker at home, and then buzzed for the flight attendant. He thought he would request that the captain radio the Toronto ground office to see if they could contact the Indian consulate with his request for a temporary extension approval by telex.

Jag explained his idea to the flight attendant, a smart-looking Quebecois woman, who then took his papers and headed to the cockpit. Jag was sure with his pilot's license the captain would allow him to come to the cockpit.

The captain was very sympathetic. As soon as Jag walked into the cockpit he extended his hand and said, "I am very sorry to hear your sad news."

Jag was impressed with the captain's gesture and shook hands with him, "Thank you."

"How can I help you?" The captain continued with his politeness. At the same time he pulled down the jump seat for Jag. "Please sit."

Jag squeezed himself in the small jump seat and proceeded to tell him his dilemma. After listening to Jag patiently, the captain summarized his story, "You want me to call our Toronto ground control, ask them to contact the Indian consulate and request an extension of your passport, if possible, by telex."

"Yes! Then I can pick it up from the Air Canada counter and continue to India."

The captain put his headset on and played with a few radio frequencies. Perhaps he was trying to reach someone on the private Air Canada channel to have a quiet talk. Jag had not seen a Boeing 727 cockpit before and he got lost in looking around. The co-pilot gave him a smile and a nod. Jag returned his nod with silent acknowledgement. He noticed that the captain had his expired Indian passport and his pilot's license in his hand.

The Toronto Ground control was contacted and the captain reiterated Jag's story. He spelled Jag's name phonetically, in aviation language, and gave them his passport number. He reminded them to get back to him as soon as possible. He turned to Jag and handed him his papers. "Well let's hope that the Indian consulate approves your request."

Jag was moved with his professionalism and empathy. "I really appreciate your help in this matter."

"Not at all, at least I am able to help as one pilot to another. You can stay here till we get the answer from Toronto. Hope the jump seat is not too uncomfortable."

"Thank you. I am fine." Jag nodded in a polite gesture.

The plane was on autopilot and the co-pilot was monitoring. The weather was clear and nice. Jag felt happy to be sitting there, watching all the instruments instead of sitting in the passenger cabin.

A few minutes later the captain was talking through his headset. Jag could not hear the conversation, but made out that it was about him. He turned to Jag and said, "The Indian Consulate can't extend your passport over the phone. They need a new application, a fee and new photos. It'll take at least three days to get a new passport in Toronto. But they said that you can continue your travel and get it renewed in India."

"How can I continue travel on an expired passport?" Jag felt angry at the consulate's lack of concern. "I have to go to New York and then catch Air India from there."

"Do you have your Canadian Citizenship card with you?" The captain tried to be helpful. Jag nodded. "Then just show that in New York. As a Canadian Citizen you don't need to show your passport in the U.S."

"But what about boarding on Air India in New York?" Jag felt helpless with the captain's solution. He changed his mind about captain's professionalism.

"You can tell your story to the Air India staff and they may let you go, or wait in New York for a new passport." The captain shrugged his shoulders. He was still polite while telling Jag the facts.

Jag got off the jump seat, "Thanks."

Captain smiled back. "Good luck."

Jag returned to his seat and worried more than before. He wondered if he should stay in Toronto and apply for a new passport, or if he should continue and try his luck in New York. If he was not allowed to travel further, then he could try there. His mind went through all sorts of possibilities. Finally, he made up his mind to just continue with his plans till he was stopped. "Mother expired" telex copy should do the trick. He knew the Indian psyche, and kept his faith in that.

He made it to the Air India counter at J.F.K. airport. He presented the passenger agent his ticket and his Indian passport. The agent, a middle-aged Indian man, just glanced at his passport photo and returned it to him with the boarding pass. Jag was very relieved.

After he got all his papers from the agent, he asked, "Do we get off in London or the same airplane continues to Delhi?"

"You'll not be allowed to get off the airplane in London; it is only one hour forty-five minutes stop." The agent sounded a bit miffed, he wanted him to move on so that he could tend to another passenger.

"Thank you," Jag said hurriedly and moved away from the counter. He felt happy that he wouldn't have to worry about the customs and immigration in London.

The final test came when he arrived in Delhi, the Palam airport as it was called at the time. He had four hours to get out of there and go to the domestic side to catch the flight for Calcutta. Jag felt happy to put his feet down inside the Palam airport's terminal building. The building was small and always crowded. He stood in a long queue for his immigration process. He knew this would be his last hurdle to cross. After this he'd be home free.

At the immigration booth he put his Indian passport and his return ticket on the counter and greeted the agent in Hindi, "*Namaste.*"

The agent was polite and said '*Namaste*' back to Jag in an official tone, and started to look through his passport to see what countries he had visited, and asked, "Purpose of your visit?"

Jag made his voice as sad as possible and said, "Mother expired."

With that the agent tried to find a blank page to stamp the passport and let him go. But then he started to flip through his passport again, and noticed the date of expiry. "Sorry sir, your passport has expired, I can't let you in."

Jag quickly pulled out the telex copy and showed him and pleaded, "See, sir, I got this telegram 'Mother expired' and I did not even check my passport and just came. What would you do if you had gotten a telegram like this?"

"I am sorry I can't do anything, you have to discuss this with the supervisor, when he comes." His tone had become very stern and official. He waved a police *Havildar* and mumbled to him something that Jag could not hear. The police officer came around, got hold of his hand, and told him to come with him.

Once more Jag tried, "What about my passport?"

Without any eye contact the agent answered, "I'll send it to the supervisor. You go with him."

The policeman took him into a corner office where there was a jail cell just like the ones Jag had seen in movies. The policeman put him in the cell and locked it. Jag was so dumbfounded he didn't know what to do or say. He had never been in a jail and now he was locked up.

"I have a flight to catch for Calcutta in two hours. I have to be home for my mother's funeral." Jag said to the policeman.

"I can't do anything till *sahib* comes in. He'd decide your fate." The *Havildar* sat on a stool and ignored him.

Jag wondered if he should have tried to bribe the immigration agent, or perhaps this policeman. But he had never bribed anybody, and he did not even know how to do that. He thought he would wait for *sahib* and deal with him. He asked the policeman again, "What time your *sahib* comes in?"

The *Havildar* gave Jag an annoyed look as if he was bothering him unnecessarily and said, "In about an hour."

From his past experiences Jag knew that Government officers were never on time. He was sure he would miss his flight to Calcutta. He sat on the bench in the cell. He was the only one in this jail and it was very quiet. Soon the *Havildar* started to snore on his stool. Jag stayed focused on the slow-moving hand of the clock. He started to wonder if coming back to India in such a rush was a rational thing to do. He worried and argued with himself in the silence of the cell then, surprisingly, fell sleep. Perhaps it was due to the jetlag or perhaps his mind refused to be overburdened with any more worries. Either way, sleep overtook him and, for the first time since he got the telex, there was oblivion.

In fifty-five minutes from the time Jag was locked up in the cell, a burly looking Sikh man in police uniform walked in. He was around fifty, with at tightly wrapped black and white beard and khaki turban. The *Havildar* woke up in a hurry and saluted him. The Sikh threw a quick glance at Jag and walked in to his small office next to the cell. The *Havildar* followed him.

Jag could hear a few words in a hushed voice. Five minutes passed by and nobody came out. Jag looked at his watch and wondered if he would be able to make it to the domestic terminal to catch the Calcutta flight. Finally he shouted out, "Hello, please."

The *Havildar* came out first and gave Jag an angry glance. He was followed by the Sikh officer who approached Jag's cell. Jag quickly pulled out the "Mother Expired" telex from his pocket and through the bars passed it to him.

"Sir, you see, I got this telegram 'Mother Expired' and, without realizing that my passport has expired, I took the first flight home. Sir, if you had received such a telegram what would you had done if you were living abroad?" Jag tried to make his English as Hindilish as possible.

The Sikh Officer took the telex from Jag's hand through the bars, and gave a thorough examination to confirm his story as true and genuine.

"I am the first son sir, and tomorrow is *Chautha* - the fourth day of the funeral of my mother. I must attend that." For the first time, Jag felt emotional saying the word *Chautha*. It was as though the word held some magic and could unlock whatever it was that he had buried in his heart. "I have to catch the Calcutta flight in one hour. Please have sympathy with my case."

The Sikh officer returned the telex to Jag and looked him in eye. "I am sorry to hear your news," he spoke in heavily Punjabi-accented English. Then he turned to the *Havildar* and ordered him, "Find Jag Sahib's luggage and then take him to the domestic terminal, and make sure he is on the flight to Calcutta."

The *Havildar* obediently answered in Hindi, "Yes sir," and unlocked the cell.

Jag approached the Sikh, "Thank you *Sardarji*," and bowed his head in respect. "And what about my passport?"

"We are going to keep that. You have to apply for a new one in Calcutta." The Sikh became a police officer again.

"But they may refuse to give me a new one, without returning the old one." Jag tried to plead.

"Don't worry, we will send it to them. Now you get going if you want to catch your plane."

Jag rushed out with the *Havildar* to get his luggage and catch his flight to Calcutta. He thought he may have to bribe somebody in Calcutta to get a new passport, but he did not want to think about it; he was relieved to be free.

The flight to Calcutta and the train journey to his home town were easy. His family was very surprised to see him arriving so fast all the way from Canada. They did not expect him to get there so soon. Some of Jag's sisters who lived in North India had not arrived yet.

All went well with the funeral, Jag thought. He never worried about his passport till the funeral was over. He started to think of his return to Canada. He called a resourceful friend in Calcutta to check how long it would take (and how much a bribe he would have to pay) to get an Indian passport in a hurry. His friend informed him after some inquiries that his contact in the passport office told him it would take a minimum one month and around ten thousand rupees of bribe money to get a new passport.

"Why so long?" Jag cried.

"This is India, *yaar* - my dear friend, not Canada. One has to go through the police check and ration card etc. to confirm your residency." The friend answered with a chuckle on Jag's naïveté.

"Why ration card?" Jag still did not understand his friend's chuckled answer.

"To confirm you live here. You want an Indian passport; you have to prove you are a citizen of India, and you live here."

Jag pondered his friend's answer and suddenly his reality hit him. "But I am no longer a citizen of India," he mumbled.

"What?" His friend shouted louder than the loud phone conversation Indians normally have.

"I have taken a Canadian Citizenship that makes me a non-citizen in India."

"Then apply for a Canadian Passport, problem solved!" Jag's friend washed his hands of the problem. Then he continued, "Oh by the way Jag, my friend at the passport office suggested that you make a police report that you have lost your passport. That will make it easier to get a new one."

Jag tried to explain, "But it was taken by a police officer at the Delhi Airport, and he said he'd send it to the passport office in Calcutta."

Jag's friend felt annoyed, he almost yelled at him "Jag how come you have become more dumb by going to Canada, don't you know how things work in India? Here the left hand does not know what the right hand is doing. Ok? Just come to Calcutta and I'll get you a lost passport police report, you take that to the Canadian embassy and get your passport there and get out of here. Clear? Understood?"

Jag felt he better not annoy his friend anymore or he may not help him. "Okay I'll come to Calcutta in the morning by Coal Mine Express train."

"Good, I'll pick you up at the Howrah station, and get everything sorted out for you by the evening."

Jag got in his friend's car at Howrah station the next morning.

"Jag tell me one thing, what right do you have to live better than me when you have not become any smarter by going to Canada?"

Jag did not understand his friend's question, "What do you mean?"

114

"You've lost all your Indian street smarts. You talk like a dumb American coming to India for the first time. Don't you remember how things work here?"

Jag accepted the insult and kept quiet.

"I have bought a nice bottle of whiskey for the police inspector and here is the envelope with some money for him. It's all set. You just sign the report and you'll have a copy; and give these presents to him. We'll be done in no time."

"So I am supposed to go to the Canadian Embassy with this police report and tell them I have lost my passport and they'll issue me a new Canadian passport. Yeah?"

"Yes *Massa*." His friend tried to mimic the American accent. "Don't you have a niece who works at the Canadian Embassy; why don't you call and tell her about everything and see if she can do something about this?"

Jag thought, yes he has lost his Indian street smarts. He did not even remember that his niece Monica worked at the Canadian Embassy. He thought he should call her and tell her the whole story. Perhaps she can find all the information in advance.

"Yes, you are right, I should call Monica. She'd be at the embassy right now." Jag shook his head in an agreeable way.

"Good, let's go to my office and book a trunk-call to her. Hope you have her office number?"

"Yes, but I don't have her extension."

"Ah we will find her. That way Canadians are quite prompt." Jag's friend looked at him and smiled.

"Thank you for the compliment," Jag smiled.

"The compliment was not for you. You actually have become dumber after going to Canada." His friend continued to insult him. This was also an Indian way of showing true friendship.

In a way, Jag's friend was right. Jag had felt helpless in India after going to Canada. In this overpopulated country everybody was impatient to get ahead and, if one was not ready to push, he was left behind. He realized that without his friend's help he would be standing at the back of a long queue, still waiting for his turn.

From his office, Jag's friend booked a trunk call to Delhi to Monica's dept. Then he called a telephone operator and told him his booking number. The call was connected immediately. Jag remembered that most business people bribed the telephone operators on a monthly basis to get their phone calls connected faster.

Jag's friend took over the phone and located Monica's extension and told her the whole story about Jag's passport fiasco at Delhi airport. He emphasized that she must do everything in her power to get her uncle a new Canadian passport, and then he handed the phone to Jag.

When Jag said hello to his niece Monica, all she asked was, "When are you coming to Delhi?"

"Hopefully tonight or tomorrow."

"Ok, I will find out about the passport and call you back in a couple of hours." Monica sounded more like a Canadian official than his favourite niece. This disappointed Jag but he decided to let it go.

Jag's friend left him in his office while he attended to his work. Alone now, Jag started to worry. What if he could not get a Canadian passport? Would he be stuck in India? Could he ever possibly live here again? He felt scared in his old country. He closed his eyes and tried to push his thoughts from his head. But they didn't leave him.

After a few minutes of silence the phone rang and his friend walked in with a big smile. "See I told you *sub theek ho jayega* - everything will be fine. Monica is on the phone for you."

"Hello, Uncle. The passport lady said if you have your Canadian citizenship card with you, and a police report that you have lost your old passport then we can issue you a temporary passport in a day. There will be no problems."

Jag loved the words 'no problems.'

"Yes I have all the documents," he said excitedly.

"Great, I'll bring the passport application with me home. We need to get it signed by a doctor as a guarantor and two new photographs."

"Ok, I'll try to get the afternoon flight for Delhi. I want to get out of India as soon as possible."

"What is the rush? Relax Uncle, for a few days in Delhi with us." Monica did not sound so official now.

"Ok, I'll see you this evening. Bye." Jag finally felt relieved as he hung up the phone.

Jag's friend had a big grin. "Ok you are buying me a big lunch now. Give me your airline tickets and I'll send the peon to the airline office to book your seat."

"Do you think your peon will be able to do that?" Jag questioned.

"My peon has more street smarts than you Mr. Jag Mohan." His friend insulted him again.

Jag meekly pulled out his airlines tickets and handed them to his friend.

The next morning Jag took all of his documents and his return airline ticket to the Canadian Embassy. The Nepali guard on the main front gate let his niece Monica in after checking her ID card, but had to phone his superior to see if he could let an Indo-Canadian, with a Canadian citizenship card as ID, into the embassy. It irritated Jag, but he kept his mouth shut. He needed a Canadian passport urgently. Finally, the guard came out of his booth and let Jag in.

With the help of Monica all the paperwork was processed very easily. A white grey-haired lady named Mrs. Mukherjee took Jag to her little room. Monica waved him bye and went to her department.

"Do you plan to travel tonight to Canada Mr. Jag Mohan?" Mrs. Mukherjee asked in a perfect Canadian English accent.

"Yes Madam, if it's possible." Jag tried to sound as Canadian as he could.

"Ok, let's try to get your passport issued fast. It may take a couple of hours. It'll be temporary for three months and then a permanent one will be mailed to your Canadian address."

"That will be fine." Jag was exceedingly polite.

"Would you mind paying the fee in Canadian dollars? I hope you have twenty dollars."

Jag immediately took a twenty-dollar bill out from his wallet. Mrs. Mukherjee put the twenty-dollar bill in her purse; took out some Indian rupees and attached them to Jag's passport application.

Jag tried not to show his surprise.

Mrs. Mukherjee said, "Fine, you can come back in 2 hours and your passport should be ready."

"Can I just wait in the lobby here? "Jag did not want to tell her that he rather not hassle with the Nepali guard at the gate again.

"That will be fine. There is a small library on the side; you can catch up with all the Canadian news there." With that Mrs. Mukherjee went inside of the embassy doors.

That night, on the plane, Jag relaxed and wondered why he was so worried about everything. After all, as his friend had said, *sub theek ho jayega.*

RASHID AND HIS RICKSHAW

Jag Mohan was suffocating. He had only been home for three days and still he felt like an outsider. It surprised him that the transition from his adopted world to his childhood world was so difficult. He blamed the grieving, but inwardly he knew that the physical distance had removed him emotionally from both his past and his family.

The small family house was already crowded with guests arriving for his mother's funeral. There was crying and wailing. Strangers and people from his past offered condolences. Jag was overcome with guilt for not being able to cry out loud for his mother's passing. He had not felt sad during the entire flight from Edmonton to Calcutta, but perhaps that was only because he was preoccupied about his expired passport. He assumed that he might feel the loss once he arrived in his small town in West Bengal. But the weight of loss did not descend upon him.

Perhaps Jag felt isolated. Living in Canada for almost seven years now had made him a stranger to his old culture. Whatever the reason, he could no longer bear the claustrophobic ritual.

And it was going to last thirteen days! God, he needed to get out of the house, just get away from the loud wailings every time a new guest arrived at the house.

"I need to get some air," Jag told his number six sister, the youngest in the family. His sister, who seemed to be managing the household throughout this time of tragedy, looked hard into his face. Seeing that he was not in need of emotional support, she nodded her head in that Indian way, moving it from side to side like a bobble. He wanted to smile at her gesture, remembering how his Canadian friends used to mimic the nod and make fun of him, but the protocol of the funeral stopped him from smiling at such time. He was supposed to look stern and sad for all thirteen days of funeral. It was expected.

Jag came out through the smelly thin gully with the open sewer and walked to the main road. He seemed to see his small town for the first time. He found the whole roundabout in front of his house very dirty and crowded. He wondered if it had always been that way. Perhaps the road had not changed at all and only his view of it had. There were more *thelewalas,* cart vendors selling fruit and vegetables, than he remembered, by the side of the road. Jag had to walk in the middle of the road, between *tongas*, with the terrible smell of horse manure, the crowded look of bicycle rickshaws, and the harsh sound of lots of cars constantly honking.

There were no pedestrian road signs, as there were in Canada. He felt lost on the very street where he had spent most of his childhood. He was torn between the discomfort of the house and the unfamiliarity of his hometown street: Should he continue for a walk or go back to the house?

Jag was standing still, undecided, when a rickshaw pulled in front of him and the driver jumped off from his seat saluting him and saying, in a Hindu greeting, *"Ram-ram Jag sahib."* Jag realized the driver knew him as he had just addressed him with his name. Though his face looked familiar, Jag could not quite remember him. Jag looked at him up and down: a narrow face with a stubble beard, a thin body, dressed in a short checkered shirt and a *lungi* - the Muslim sarong-type wraparound - very dilapidated rubber chapels, and bony legs.

The rickshaw driver understood immediately that Jag was having problems remembering him. Poor Indians have a knack of recognizing such things very quickly.

"I am Rashid. I used to live behind your house in the hut. I used to be your kite runner, when we used to have kite wars."

Jag remembered his childhood kite war days, and remembered young Rashid's very happy face with his huge smile. Rashid was the fastest runner in the neighborhood. He had been Jag's side-kick forever. Jag would let him hold his *chakra* - the roller wheel of kite, when the sky was clear and there was no threat of attack. Jag handled all the kite wars himself with Rashid standing beside him, advising him occasionally. If Jag lost the war and his kite was cut off, then Rashid would run to grab the loose kite. Among so many kids running to grab the loose kites Rashid always seemed to get to Jag's kite first to bring it back to him. Sometimes there were fights among the kids, but Rashid was never a part of it. He was too fast.

Jag remembered his kite war lieutenant with very warm memories. *"Ram-ram Rashid."* Immediately, he realized his mistake and corrected it by saying, *"Salam wale kum Rashid"* - a Muslim greeting. And then he extended his hand.

Rashid shied away from shaking Jag's hand. He knew his boundaries; he could not shake hands with his foreign educated friend. Instead he saluted him again and repeated, *"Ram-ram Jag Sahib."*

Then, suddenly, Rashid's eyes became wet and with a sad low voice he expressed his condolences to Jag in his uneducated childhood language, "So sad - Ma-ji passed away so suddenly." Tears started to roll from Rashid's eyes. He bent down and grabbed the corner of his *lungi*-wrap to wipe them.

Jag noticed that Rashid was not wearing underwear. He could see his private parts. He turned his eyes to his old friend's face. Rashid was blowing his nose in his *lungi*.

"It's Allah's wish, Rashid." Jag did not say, "It's Bhagwan's wish." Canada had taught him to be sensitive to other people's culture and language. Jag had learned a lot about multiculturalism. He continued to console Rashid, "At least she did not suffer too long. Can you imagine Ma-Ji living half-paralyzed? She would have made everybody's life a hell."

It was the first time since arriving that he talked of his mother's passing. Not his sisters, not his adult friends and not the household of many mourners could touch that place in his heart. But here, his childhood friend, his kite-runner, held the key to what was locked in his heart. He was filled with a bittersweet sadness.

Rashid nodded and smiled. All of Jag's friends knew his mother's 'go-go-go' nature. She never could sit idle, even at the age of sixty-seven. Jag patted Rashid's back and climbed into his rickshaw.

"Just take me anywhere Rashid. I want to *pehchan* - reacquaint myself with this town."

Jag did not want to bargain or argue with a fare today with his old kite-runner friend. He was doing 'quite well' in Canada and the dollar went a long way in Indian rupees. He thought he would be generous with Rashid today. He needed to undo some of his guilt and sadness by helping an old, famished friend.

Climbing onto his seat, Jag's old friend commented, "Jag sahib you speak a funny Hindi now."

Jag curiously asked, "What do you mean?"

Rashid did not hesitate clarifying, "You speak Hindi like an *Angrez* - an English-sahib now."

In mock anger Jag tried to mimic his childhood accent and ordered him, "Okay, you stop calling me sahib then and I'll speak in local Hindi."

They both chuckled at their little exchange and Rashid bobbled his head from side to side in the Indian way.

Rashid slowly started to pedal his rickshaw. Jag got lost in his old memories. His mother used to shout at the end of the day to Rashid's hut and he would come running to get all the leftovers. Jag's parents used to argue about her cooking too much food and extra going to waste. But she purposely did this so that she could give away some of it to Rashid's family. This was her way of doing a good deed everyday. Jag remembered there were a lot of Rashid's sisters, brothers and cousins who lived in that little hut that Jag could see from the back window of his house.

Jag got tired of looking around. He could not recall any of the places. The town had grown. Streets had become very busy. He moved forward on his seat so he could talk to Rashid. "I did not see any huts at the back of the house - where do you and your family live now?"

Rashid answered without any complaints. "The government threw us out of there. It was their land. Now we live in the beggar's colony near the railway station."

Jag thought of how he had seen a new slum area when he was coming from the railway station to his house on a rickshaw.

Rashid started to sweat. His under-nourished - no, almost famished - body was glistening with sweat. Jag felt guilty sitting in the back. Then he remembered that this was how Rashid made his living every day. It's easy to understand poverty in India and to adjust to it.

"So Rashid do you have a family?"

"Yes, I have a wife and five daughters. My oldest is almost marriageable age; she is going be ten in two months."

"Marriage at ten?" Jag knew that such things happened in India, but he had temporarily forgotten or, perhaps, he was hoping that perhaps India had changed.

"Don't you send them to school?" Jag pursued.

"How can I sahib? I barely make enough money to feed them. And why send girls to school? They are going to get married and go to different families to labour there. Now, if I had a son then perhaps I'd have sent him to at least primary school."

"But things are changing; people are sending their daughters to school. These days daughters are doing as well as sons."

"Maybe in your foreign countries. Here in India people still ask for big dowries and burn their daughter-in-law if she does not bring enough cash. Jag-sahib it'll take a long time for the poor of India to improve."

Rashid was almost out of breath. The road was slightly uphill. He stood up on his pedals to keep going, till he could no longer and then he got off and pulled the rickshaw. Jag offered to get off and walk with him, but Rashid insisted that he stay sitting. He finally made it to the top, wiped his sweat with his *lungi* and climbed again on his rickshaw.

When the road was downhill he did not have to pedal too hard. Rashid continued the conversation. "My wife thinks the oldest is already too old for marriage, but what can I do, I cannot save any money to marry her off."

"How much do you earn from this rickshaw every day?" In India, people are blunt about asking *how-much-do-you-earn*? Jag had been asked many times the same question but he learned to always give the Canadian evasive answer, "I am doing fine."

Rashid's answer was honest, "I have to pay ten rupees to the owner of the rickshaw every day for twelve hours. Anything above I earn is mine. Some days it is ten, some days it's fifteen rupees." Jag calculated quickly into dollars. Rashid was earning less than a dollar per day.

"How do you live on so little?" Jag did not seem genuine. He knew he should be more aware; one must not forget one's roots by changing countries.

"Oh, we manage. Sometimes we eat only one meal a day. Ma-Ji, Allah bless her soul, was very kind. She always gave food to us at night."

Jag kept quiet at the mention of his mother. He looked around. They were heading out of town. He remembered that there was a Muslim *dargah* on that road, and they used to celebrate a huge *Urs* festival once a year. *Qawwals* from all over the country used to visit and sing Sufi songs in praise of the *Pir Baba*. Jag, as a child, used to love the qawwali singing. All the Hindus and Muslim took part in these things together. Jag's mother, Ma-ji, used to always remind him to bring the offerings from the *dargah* on their frequent visits.

"Are we going to Pir Baba's *dargah*?" Jag asked.

"Yes, I thought we go pray for Ma-Ji there."

Jag had already had enough of praying and grieving for three days at home. He did not want any more of it. But Rashid's tone of voice pleaded him to do it one more time with him. Against his wishes, Jag silently continued.

The *dargah* was not very far, and it was downhill all the way. Rashid was relaxed. The rickshaw kept rolling on its own and the wind helped him to dry his sweat. They made it there in no time.

Rashid parked his rickshaw in a stand and asked another driver to look after it as they were going in for a prayer. The other driver, half-dozed as he waited for his customer to come back, nodded silently.

As soon as Jag got off the rickshaw a few kids surrounded him and tried to sell flowers and *chadors* for the prayers. Rashid shushed, *chalo-chalo*, them away. Jag quietly passed Rashid a fifty-rupees note, saying, "You decide how you want to do this prayer and buy whatever you need."

Rashid gave him a curious look.

Jag immediately answered the look, "This is your prayer and you do it your way. I am just going to watch."

Rashid managed to get some flowers, a small *chador* and two head scarves for them for less than fifteen rupees. He bargained even in a place of prayer! The *dargah* was not very crowded, so they did not have to stand in the line anywhere.

Like Rashid, Jag tied the scarf on his head, while Rashid raised his hand to an approaching Mullah, saying very politely, "We're here for a very quiet prayer. We don't need your help."

The Mullah looked at Jag expecting he'd change his mind, but Jag looked back at him blankly.

Jag followed Rashid into the *dargah*, where Pir baba's *mazar* - graveyard was. Rashid put the small chador on top of the *mazar* and then spread some flowers on it. He gave Jag some flowers and waved him to do the same. Then he bent down and prayed. Jag followed Rashid in everything he was doing. Rashid's face was very solemn. After a few minutes he got up and circled the *mazar* a few times. Then they slowly walked outside backwards without showing their backs to the *mazar*.

"I prayed to Allah to take care of Ma-Ji and send her to heaven." Rashid said with a smile. Jag smiled back nodding.

They came out of the *dargah*. Jag saw a cement bench under a tree and a watermelon-selling cart near it. He proposed to Rashid, "Let's sit down here and have some watermelon."

Rashid bobbled his head from side to side meaning "Okay."

Jag bought two big pieces of watermelon and gave one to Rashid, tilting his head with an eye signal to Rashid to pay for it. Both men knew the vendor would charge Jag double the price. They sat on the bench and quietly started to eat. The watermelon was very juicy and sweet. Juice ran all over Jag's hands and dropped on his shirt. Rashid smiled at him. Jag thought he had forgotten how to eat things on the street. He took out some paper napkins from his pocket - a Canadian habit of carrying them in India, and passed a couple to Rashid. Rashid was not used to this luxury of wiping with paper napkins, so he watched Jag.

Jag and Rashid sat sharing their grief. He felt Rashid was grieving more for his mother than he was. Jag wished he could grieve for his mother as openly as Rashid seemed to. He couldn't help but resent the poor man. He had left the house to escape the guilt and the suffocation and here he was, outside in the open air, suffocating. It was time to change the subject.

"Rashid, how much does a rickshaw like yours cost?" Jag started thinking about helping his childhood friend, after all, he was doing 'quite well' in Canada. But more than that, he felt the need to do a good deed while he was grieving. It is a Hindu thing to do a *pind-dan* - a donation when one's parent passes away. A suggestion made by a Pundit during the daily prayers at home, expecting the donation would come to him.

"My Seth, the owner of the rickshaw, has been trying to sell me that one with the license for four thousand rupees, but I can't afford even the marriage of my own daughter. It is beyond my means," Rashid did not feel any shame in admitting his poverty.

Jag calculated the amount in dollars. He felt he should buy the rickshaw for Rashid. He didn't want any glory. He only felt all this was part of his duty to mankind and, besides, he felt guilty because he had been able to escape poverty. For Jag, Canada was not the land of milk and honey, but the land of enormous waste. He could spend more than the cost of a rickshaw on a dinner date alone.

Besides, Jag thought, the funeral Pundit had advised him to do a *pind-dan*. What's better than helping an old friend? Let the fat Pundit go to hell! Jag smiled at the thought.

Rashid finished eating his watermelon and carefully wiped his mouth and fingers with the paper napkin as if he did not want to destroy it. He wanted to preserve it as long as possible. Jag watched his carefulness.

"Ok, Rashid, go see your Seth and make the deal and we will buy that rickshaw tomorrow morning."

"But I can't afford it. I will not be even able to pay it back to you. I can't accept such a gift from you," Rashid hesitated.

"Don't worry; you don't have to pay it back. It's Ma-Ji who is buying it for you. She had asked me to do this." Jag knew if he said Ma-Ji's name then Rashid would not object to the gift.

Rashid saw a smile on Jag's face. "How can Ma-Ji say that to you when you arrived here only after she passed away? May Allah bless her."

"Oh, she asked number six sister to tell me that before she died." Jag made up the story.

Rashid happily felt defeated. How could he disobey Ma-Ji's last wish? "Okay I'll go see Seth and ask him."

Jag headed for the rickshaw, "Let's get back home before the Pundit starts thinking I am missing my duties."

Rashid felt happy for the first time in his adult life. He did not have problems pedaling uphill. He kept on chattering. "You can't ride on anybody's else rickshaw for the rest of your days here."

Jag acknowledged. "Hunh."

"And I'm going to take your younger brother's kids to school, everyday. No use giving that money to another rickshaw driver. He does not have to pay me anything."

"Hunh."

"Then I'm going to rent the rickshaw at night and save all that money for you. When you come back, I'll give that money back to you."

Jag did not care about his repayment. "You first take care of your daughters, and then worry about saving for me." Jag was feeling at peace with the thought of doing a good deed in his mother's name. And he was happy that he could help his childhood kite-runner friend.

Rashid's chatter continued, "I think I am going to give the rickshaw a name."

"Name? What sort of a name for a rickshaw?" Jag became curious.

"Oh, you will see. Like other driver owners give names to their rickshaw - *Meri-Anarkali* or *Ram ke Naam* - My Beloved or In the Name of God."

Jag had seen such silly names painted at the back of rickshaws. Some drivers preferred calling their rickshaw by name like *Meri-Anarkali,* rather than just simply saying 'It's my rickshaw.' The name made their rickshaw personal. Some even had pasted pictures of different gods and put incense on them first thing in the morning. The nostalgia was overwhelming as Jag slowly started to remember his forgotten India.

"What sort of a name?" Jag repeated his question to Rashid. By now he was at the top of the hill and he did not have to pedal so hard.

Rashid turned on his seat and looked at Jag with a smile. "Wait, you will see."

"Ok. I'll wait."

Rashid headed downhill and started to hum a Hindi film-song. Jag got lost in his old home town scenery.

Rashid pulled in the rickshaw right near the gully of Jag's house. He unwrapped his *lungi* from the waist side and took out all the change from Jag's fifty-rupee note he had given him at the dargah. "Here is the leftover change from the fifty."

Jag did not touch it. "You keep that. That's your fare."

"No, no! That's too much."

"Take the afternoon off. Buy something for your wife and daughters. We will go see your Seth tomorrow morning at ten. Is that okay? The Canadian-ism popped out of Jag.

Rashid shook his head in the Indian way to say, "Yes."

Next morning, right at 10:00, Rashid showed up at the house very happy and excited. He was wearing a new shirt and a clean *lungi*. As soon as Jag came out he saluted and said his usual greetings, "*Ram-ram*, Jag sahib."

Jag made a mock angry face at him, "Stop this Sahib thing, I am an Indian, not an *Angrez*."

Rashid followed Jag to his rickshaw on the street, nattering, "But big rich people here like to be called sahib, even though they are not *Angrez*."

Sitting on the rickshaw, Jag retorted, "Fine call them Sahibs, but not me. Ok?"

Rashid bobbled his head.

"What did your Seth say about selling of the rickshaw?"

Rashid started to pedal towards the main market on Burra Bazar street. "He does not think you will show up or bring the money."

Jag felt surprised, "Why?"

"He says all these rich NRIs come from abroad and promise a moon to poor people here and then disappear."

The comment pinched Jag. Yes, he thought, perhaps he had become an NRI, a Non-resident Indian, but still he would like to think that he was different!

"Maybe it's partially true, but he should not generalize such things."

Rashid was still high on his emotions. "I told the Seth that you're not like that and you're from here and we grew up together," he said. Jag felt good that Rashid defended him.

Seth had a small bicycle and rickshaw repair shop on the Burra Bazar Street. He owned a few rickshaws that he rented out to drivers on a daily-rate basis. It was hard for the poor drivers to get a rickshaw license from the Town Municipality. So Seth controlled the market. He was not a bad man, just a shrewd businessman.

Seth was a tall, thin, balding man, with glasses and a big *Chandan tikka* on his forehead. He was a religious man who went to the temple every morning. A great bushy mustache balanced his lack of hair on his balding head. He sat on a nice old cushioned chair looking after his long Indian-style ledger books.

When he saw Jag walking in with Rashid, he immediately knew who he was. Seth stood up and put his hands up in a *Namaste,* the traditional Indian greeting. Jag also wished him a *Namaste* and then extended his hand to shake with him. Seth warmly shook his hand.

Seth shouted to one his young boy mechanics, "Aire' clean this chair quickly for Jag Sahib." The boy ran and wiped the chair across from the table with his greasy rag and then ran back to fix his bicycle.

Seth gestured to Jag to sit on the chair. Jag took out a paper napkin from his pocket and wiped the chair again, while Rashid squatted on the floor. Jag wanted to get on with the business as soon as possible. No time to waste! But, in India, things go much slower than in Canada. Before he could start any conversation, Seth shouted at the young boy again, "Ramu, go get a couple of special *chais* and some hot samosas from the next door." Jag tried to stop him but Seth waved the boy to go.

"I am very sorry to hear your mother's expiry." Seth expressed his condolences to Jag.

"Yes, that's why I am here. This rickshaw is sort of a *dan* from my mother to Rashid. I have known him since we were kids," Jag tried to move the conversation from formalities to the business at hand.

Seth was not in any hurry, "Lucky Rashid. Now he will be rich." He smiled at Rashid, who obligingly returned a smile to Seth and Jag, while shaking his head. Seth continued to Jag, "You live in Canada now?"

Jag did not want such personalized talk, but that is the way things work in India, so he nodded to him in the same way as Rashid had nodded. Jag was having fun mimicking his old habits.

"And you do own your business there?" Seth continued his query.

Jag bobbled his head again from side to side.

"What sort of business?"

Now Jag had to answer him, he could not just shake his head, "I have an air taxi business. I am a pilot, now. It is like you having a rickshaw rental business here. The difference is that I fly my own airplanes."

Seth seemed suitably impressed with Jag. Maybe he was thinking that had he known this before, he could have raised the selling price of the rickshaw. Even though Jag had been living abroad, he could sense these thoughts on Seth's face. He even sensed Seth's next question.

"So you must be earning a lot?"

"I am comfortable."

Ramu brought in two milky sweet teas in glasses covered with plates and two samosas on dry leaves plates, on a tray. Seth helped him put one tea and a samosa on the table in front of Jag, and the other for himself. Nothing was offered to Rashid.

Jag passed his samosa and tea to Rashid, lying to Seth politely, "You know during the thirteen days of funeral prayers, I am not supposed to eat or drink outside." Mourning in India allows almost any kind of made-up lies.

Rashid hesitated but Jag forced the food on him. Seth's expression was not a happy one as Rashid took the tea and samosa.

Jag felt this would be a good time to talk to Seth about the selling price while his mouth was full. "Rashid was telling me that you want to sell the rickshaw and the license for four thousand rupees."

"No, no," his mouth half-full with samosa Seth continued, "only the rickshaw, not the license. License is extra."

Jag looked at Rashid to confirm this.

Rashid's face turned very angry. He didn't like that fact that Seth was trying to extract more money from Jag. He tried to remind him, "Seth, you told me four thousand rupees for the rickshaw and the license, both."

"No, no. You must have misunderstood me. You always make such mistakes. I told you four thousand for rickshaw and license extra." Seth spoke to him almost in a shouting tone.

Rashid was almost in tears. His dream of owning his own rickshaw was fast disappearing. Jag understood the drama. He knew he had no other choice but to bargain with Seth.

Seth happily continued with his samosa and tea. He knew he had dropped the ball in Jag's grieving court, and perhaps Jag's guilt of doing a good deed would win him a few more rupees.

"How much for the license?" Jag asked with some sort of authority.

"One thousand rupees. Cash." Seth was more experienced in such matters.

Jag looked at the sad face of Rashid. Perhaps now Rashid wanted Jag to walk away from the deal. Seth was trying to rob him blindly. Jag thought of making one last bargain with Seth.

"Ok. I'll give four thousand and five hundred, all cash, right now for both the rickshaw and the license, or I am walking." With that Jag stood up. Rashid thought the deal was gone sour so he got up too. But Jag knew Seth would take the offer; that's why he had said words 'all cash' slowly and loudly.

"Sit, sit, sir, why are you rushing like foreigners?" Seth tried to calm Jag.

Jag sat down again. Rashid kept standing, poor-man with no knowledge of such bargains.

"So you will give me ALL CASH?" Seth asked to confirm. Jag nodded.

"And no receipt?"

Jag felt he could push Seth a bit. "Of course you have to give me some kind of receipt, otherwise, how is Rashid going to register his license?"

"Don't worry about that. I will get his license registered." Seth assured.

"But you have to give me some kind of receipt."

Seth realized that he would have to give some kind of receipt to this NRI, or he might walk away. He did not want to lose a profitable cash deal.

Seth waved Jag to come close so the others couldn't hear him. "I'll give you a receipt of rupees two thousand as the purchase price of rickshaw. You know how the tax system works here. Otherwise I have to pay a lot of taxes."

Jag was quite familiar with India's underground economy and black money system. So he nodded yes. He pulled a bundle of new one hundred rupee notes from his pocket and started to count. "I am going to give you two thousand rupees now and you give me a receipt, and the rest I will pay when the license is registered."

Seth objected, "You should pay me full amount now. I said I will get the license registered."

Jag stayed firm putting two thousand rupees in front of him, "Two thousand now and rest when the license is done."

Seth unhappily started to count the money. After he was finished counting, Jag asked, "How long will it take to get the license transferred?"

"About a week." Seth wanted to delay as much as possible. That way he could earn more rental money on the rickshaw.

Jag was enjoying this horse-trading with Seth. He switched to his English-Hindi accent and baited Seth again. "Here is another deal for you. You get me all the license registration done today and I'll give fifty rupees extra on top of everything."

He smiled at Jag and did not take the bait, "I'll try but it's very hard. You have to bribe the clerks. I will let Rashid know."

Jag was ready to leave and then he sat down again. "How about that receipt for two thousand rupees?" he whispered to Seth.

Seth started to scribble on a small chit.

Jag protested immediately, "No, no. I want a *pukka* - genuine receipt on your letterhead."

Seth saw he was very determined about this. He pulled his letterhead out and wrote him a receipt in Hindi. Jag interrupted him, "Hope you have a one-rupee registry stamp."

Seth smiled, "You haven't forgotten anything."

As most businessmen do in India, Seth kept such things. He found a stamp and put it at the bottom of the page then signed on it. It's a poor-man's way of legalizing a receipt in India, inherited from British days. He passed it to Jag for inspection.

Jag looked at it and smiled. If he stayed a few more days in India he would be able to conduct business like locals.

Seth shouted at Rashid on their way out. "Rashid, come back after dropping Jag sahib, so we can get your registry done." Rashid shook his head to Seth and followed Jag.

Jag turned around for one final instruction to Seth, "Please register the rickshaw in Rashid's name, not mine."

Seth did not like this, nevertheless, he shrugged his shoulders as if he did not care. He was visibly jealous that Rashid was getting all this for free.

Jag was happy that he was able to finalize the deal with only an extra five hundred rupees. Rashid was unhappy that Seth had been able to squeeze an extra five hundred from Jag. Climbing onto the rickshaw Jag passed the receipt to Rashid, "Here, you better keep this. It's your rickshaw now."

Taking the paper from Jag, Rashid said angrily, "He is a thief! He steals from poor people."

"It's okay; he stole it from me, not from you. You don't need to worry about it."

Waving the paper, Rashid continued, "Yeah but this is my burden. I have to pay you back someday."

"No, you don't have to. You don't have to worry about it. Remember Ma-Ji had asked me to do this. Be happy, you got a special tea and a samosa from your Seth."

Pedaling back to Jag's home Rashid murmured, "It was a day-old samosa, re-heated. Perhaps it'll give me stomach ache now. It was full of stale potatoes."

Jag stayed quiet, letting Rashid vent out his anger.

Outside the house, Jag got off and gave Rashid a hundred-rupee note. "Here, you will need this as Seth may not give you the rickshaw for two or three days."

"No, I'll be okay." Rashid was adamant about any further burden.

Jag shoved the note in his new shirt pocket. "Go back and see if he gets the rickshaw registered today. But don't sign or thumb-print anything there. Just tell him I want to check all the papers first."

Rashid nodded. "Seth will do it today. He saw all the cash in your pocket and he will want to transfer that cash into his pocket as soon as possible. He is like that."

Finally, Rashid smiled. Jag laughed out loud and patted Rashid's back hard, the way he used to do when Rashid captured kites for him all those years ago. It was a winning pat between two childhood friends - friends who understood the game.

Number five sister was very practical in money matters and she had a sixth sense about such things. So, late in the afternoon, when Rashid showed up at the house very excited, she came to warn Jag, "Now don't go around and blow your money away and be a show off." But number five never understood the burden of a *pind-dan* - final rites, of a foreign returned brother. She only understood what the Pundit wanted done. Jag smiled quietly and walked out with Rashid.

"Seth had all the papers registered already. He wanted me to thumb-print and take them. But I told him that Jag sahib wants to check them before I do that. So now he wants to see you in a hurry." Rashid smiled with his last sentence.

Jag sat on the rickshaw and noticed Rashid's new shirt drenched in the sweat. "Were you working all morning?"

"No, Seth wanted me to go to Municipality office and get all the license papers done."

"Did you have to bribe the clerks?"

"No, all these guys are on a *hafta* from Seth." Rashid turned and smiled a you-know-what-I-mean smile. Jag smiled back, understanding.

Seth was dozing in his cushioned seat. Hearing Jag and Rashid walk in the shop, he opened his eyes and made a pretended move to stand up and greet them. Jag waved him to stay put in his seat, and sat across from him. Rashid stood behind him.

Seth was his polite best, "I told Rashid to thumb-print and take the papers. I did not want him to bother you again. But he insisted on bringing you back."

"Yes, I had told him that I'd like to pay you the rest of the sum and clear the accounts, before he takes possession of the rickshaw."

Seth gave a small laugh, "You foreign returned people are very fussy about the paperwork, aren't you?" He passed some papers to Jag.

Jag smiled back. "Yes we foreign returned people like to keep things transparent and clean." He looked at the papers; they were written in Bengali. Jag had forgotten most of it, but still could read a bit slowly. He purposely read out a few top lines to impress Seth.

"Ah, you can still read Bengali. *Wah* - Great. I can't." He seemed truly surprised.

"Then how do you know if all the papers are correct?" Jag inquired.

"I've to trust the clerks at the Municipality."

Seth looked at Rashid and sort of ordered him, "Rashid, go fetch me a tea from next door!" Then inquiringly, he looked at Jag, who shook his head without lifting his eyes from the papers.

Jag shouted back at Rashid, "Bring that receipt I gave you this morning."

Nodding Rashid walked out to fetch the tea for Seth.

"Are you donating this rickshaw to Rashid?" Seth whispered.

"Yes, this is my *pind-dan*." Jag did not whisper.

"But you give *pind-dan* to a Brahmin, a pundit. Rashid is a Muslim." Seth protested weakly.

"We do *pind-dan* to a river, a cow and a pundit, a person I hardly know. At least I know Rashid since my childhood." Then Jag got close to Seth's face and whispered to him, "Besides I am no longer a Hindu, I eat steak, beef, a holy cow, in Canada."

Seth was not sure how to respond. "But giving *pind-dan* to a Muslim is *paap* - a sin."

"And stealing from the poor is not a sin?" Jag felt annoyed and asked Seth.

Seth was too business-savvy to argue any further. Jag pulled out his hundred rupees and started to count. Silence continued between them. Rashid brought Seth's tea in a glass covered with a plate, and handed the receipt to Jag.

Jag looked for a pen on Seth's table. He wrote down at the bottom of the receipt: Received in full the price of rickshaw serial number RNG1234, (he copied it from the license papers) from Rashid Muhammad on 1st Feb. 1977.

He passed the paper to Seth, "Please sign this and I can give you the rest of the money."

Seth looked at the paper and said, "What is the need of this? I have already given you the receipt this morning."

Jag kept hold of the twenty-five hundred rupees, shaking his hand so Seth could see them, "Yes, but I noticed in these papers in Bengali, that the selling price of the rickshaw is mentioned as *ek hazzar taka* – one thousand rupees. I have only mentioned 'received in full' not the actual price of the rickshaw on this paper.

So I can insist you get me the right-priced, two thousand rupees-license papers or you sign this receipt. Or we cancel the deal and you return my money. Your choice."

Rashid heard Jag's bargain. His face was full of anger. He hated Seth at this moment. He addressed Jag, "Jag sahib, I don't want this rickshaw anymore. Cancel the deal and take your money back."

Jag smiled at Rashid. "Go have a tea outside, and eat something. I'll be out in a couple of minutes. Go, go!"

Rashid left with reluctance.

Seth wanted to get this transaction over with and quickly signed the paper and returned it to Jag. Satisfied, Jag handed him twenty-five hundred rupees in new notes. Seth put the money in his drawer without counting.

Jag saw this and smiled, "At least count it to be sure I have given you the right amount."

"Na, you will not cheat me. Don't make me anymore *sharminda* - ashamed."

Jag stood up, took the receipt and the license papers from the table. He did not want to shake hands with this man; instead he raised his hands and said *"Namaste."* Seth nodded his head the Indian way, while Jag walked out.

Rashid was sitting on his seat on the rickshaw, brooding. Jag walked and passed the papers to him. "Did you have tea?"

"Na. That Seth is a total thief."

"Okay, you go home now and celebrate with your family. Take the evening off." Jag said trying to cheer him up. "I am going to walk around in the bazaar then go home. Go, don't worry."

Rashid did not want leave Jag alone or let him walk back. Jag walked away and waved him to go from the back of his head.

The next morning, number five sister walked into Jag's room annoyed. "So you bought Rashid a rickshaw, ha?"

"How do you know?"

"He is waiting for you downstairs. He told Bhabhi - younger brother's wife, to cancel the kids' rickshaw to school; and from now on he will take them and bring them back. She told me that you bought rickshaw for Rashid."

"Yes it's my *pind-dan*."

Hearing that word, Jag's number five sister's eyes filled up with tears and she walked out of the room.

Rashid looked relaxed and happy when Jag walked up to him on the street. The rickshaw looked washed, polished and clean. He jumped off the seat and grabbed Jag's arm. "Come see this." Excitedly he took him to the back of the rickshaw.

At the back of the rickshaw there were two words painted in Hindi in red colour: *Swargiya Ma-Ji*.

"I gave the rickshaw a name; I got it painted last night." Rashid was very proud with the name.

Jag smiled at the name on the rickshaw, "Do you know the meaning of *swargiya*?"

"Yeah, the painter told me - it means 'gone to heaven.' The painter said all the rich Marwari people get the names painted like this, in the name of their late parents when they donate any property."

Jag joked, "Yeah, those rich Marawaris book their berth in heaven before they are born. What if Ma-ji did not go to heaven, instead she went to hell?"

"*Chi-chi*, how can you say a thing like that about your own mother? Where else she would go? Allah has a first-class ticket reserved for her into the heaven. I know this for sure."

Jag mimicked Rashid's nod and smiled at him. "So you told the whole town about this - I got you the rickshaw."

"No, no! I just told Bhabhi-ji that I'll take the kids to school and back from now on. No use paying somebody else. This will save her money."

"And how are you going to take care of your children if you start this free service for everybody? You should send your daughters to school. Save some money for them."

Rashid opposed the argument, "No, this is your younger brother's kids; at least, please, let me do this in return."

Jag knew he would not be able to argue with such sentimentality. He smiled again at his childhood friend. Rashid happily patted on the passenger seat, and said, "Let's go for a small ride."

Jag sat down. Rashid headed for *Pir-baba's dargah*. Jag realized he would have to go through the previous day's routine all over again, only this time it would be Rashid's prayer and offering. He did not mind.

From that day that till the thirteenth and the final day of Jag's Ma-ji's funeral, Rashid waited outside the house and would not allow Jag to walk anywhere.

After the *pind-dan*, on the thirteenth day, and feeding over one hundred people who came for the final ceremony, Jag packed some food and brought it down to Rashid. "Here, take this home and feed this to your family. This is the last meal you are going get from Ma-ji."

Rashid's eyes filled with huge tears accepting the food from Jag.

"Now don't cry. You told me Allah has a first-class seat for Ma-ji in heaven; Ma-ji is *swargiya* now, right?"

This put a smile on Rashid's face.

"Listen, Rashid, I will leave for Canada tomorrow, so if I don't see you then you be good and take care of your children. Save money for them."

"So soon? Aren't you staying a few more days?" Rashid's face became sad again.

"No, I can't. In Canada you just have to work. Not too many holidays."

"Then I'll take you to the railway station." Rashid firmly made the decision.

Jag smiled, nodded and headed back in the house.

In the evening, number six sister came to chat with Jag. She had missed him while he was away and, already, he was leaving again. She was not all financial like number five sister. Not as disapproving, either. If any of the sisters felt close to Jag, it was her. She looked around as Jag was packing his things away.

"You have become much more organized compared to when you lived here. Good. I remember packing your suitcase when you were going to Canada the first time."

Jag smiled at his little sister's reminder, "Yeah, when you live alone you've got to learn to do all this and, besides I travel almost daily as a pilot."

"Do you miss Mum?" The sudden question surprised Jag.

"Why do you ask?"

"It seems you came from Canada just to fulfill the formalities of 'attending' a mother's funeral. You did a few chores, threw some money here and there, and now you're back to your Canada. You never sat down with us and asked how Mum was in her last few days? Or how Dad is? Or how we feel? I never saw a drop of a tear coming out of your eyes. Oh well, not to worry, we will survive. Have a good trip back to your home in Canada." Her eyes filled up with tears and she walked out abruptly.

The conversation came back to haunt Jag in the airplane once he took off from London to Toronto. Then, suddenly he started to cry. Thankfully, the seat next to him was empty. He put his face down on the tray table and let his tears pour out.

As soon as Jag got back to Canada he went back to his work-work-work. Soon he forgot Rashid. Soon he forgot his mother's funeral and soon he forgot his short conversation with number six sister on the last day.

Three years passed quickly. India seemed very far away, almost a dream, until the day he received a short note from his younger brother: "Dad is not well. Perhaps you should visit us." Jag knew it was time to go home again.

Only when Jag sat on a rickshaw on the way to his house, did he remember Rashid and the rickshaw. It was early morning, and the air was full of fog and pollution. There was a slight chill in the air. People were walking around wrapped in shawls and head covers. Across the street from his house, at the rickshaw stand, he saw all the rickshaw drivers still sleeping curled up on their passenger seats.

Nobody knew about Jag's surprise visit. Soon everybody woke up, quite excited. Once again, Jag felt like a stranger in his childhood house, even though it was filled with his brother's family and even though his father was still alive. He wondered how long he could survive in the strangeness. Not back even a day and Jag could feel his throat tighten and his chest constrict.

Making the excuse of jet-lag, he went to his old room to sleep, but he could not.

Hearing his unpacking noises, Bhabhi, his younger brother's wife, brought Jag a glass of water and a cup of tea, with two Marie's biscuits on the plate.

"Is this bottled water?" Jag asked, thinking of his stomach. She shook her head 'no' and then added in a hurry, "I can ask the *Dayi* - maid, to get it from the shop. It'll take only a couple of minutes."

"Not to worry. I'll just have tea now."

She sat across from him with her head half-covered by her sari.

"Have dad and younger brother gone out?" Jag asked to get some news about the family from her. He did not communicate well with his father or younger brother. And this distance had increased since he went away to Canada.

Jag picked up the small tea cup and saw that the milk and sugar were boiled with the tea. He had stopped drinking Chai - Indian tea. He drank only black tea and coffee now. But he decided to force himself to drink this cup of chai since he was home.

"Please take a biscuit, don't drink the tea on empty stomach," she politely reminded.

Jag picked up one. As a kid he used to love these Marie's biscuits. He used to dunk them in his tea and slurp. Quite often the biscuit would become limp and drop onto his shirt. His mother used to give him heck for it, while he laughed. 'Sloppy-sloppy, now I have to wash your shirt again.' He saw his mother's colorized photo on the wall, as if she were going yell at him from there.

He turned to his younger brother's wife and asked, "How are things here?"

She nodded and said, "Okay." She always started the conversation slowly with one- or two-word answers, as though talking a lot at the start was not appropriate.

Jag felt, perhaps, he should ask about things outside of the family first. "Is Rashid still taking the kids to school in his rickshaw?" Now he knew he would get a full-sentence answer.

"He did for about a year, but after that he disappeared. I asked around but nobody gave me a proper answer," she answered in a sort of complaining way.

Jag did not know how to respond so he changed the topic again. "How is business? And what's wrong with *bhau* - dad?"

Younger brother's wife cleared her throat and was ready to give the full update, "The business is very bad, and *bhau* is getting old. He can't handle anything, and will not give full control to your brother. So they argue all the time. You know I can't say anything to either one of them," she paused to see Jag's reaction and then continued. "Perhaps you can sit down with them and resolve this between them."

Jag knew the word 'resolve' meant to help them out of their pressing financial problems. He had to see what their demands were and how much he could afford to give away. "Ok, I'll talk to them in a day or two." He forced himself to gulp the tea and got up. "I think I'll go for a walk. "

Jag was curious to find out about Rashid. He went onto the street and looked around. There was no change anywhere except that the street was even more crowded than his previous visit, three years ago.

Jag walked to the rickshaw stand. He did not recognize anybody. The drivers thought of him as a customer and surrounded him with questions, "Where to sahib?" They wanted to bargain a fare. He waved them off with a firm 'No.'

Finally, after wandering up and down looking for Rashid, Jag asked one of the older drivers, "I am looking for Rashid; he used to have a rickshaw here about three years ago. Do you know where can I find him?"

The driver seemed to remember Jag. He did not say anything, just raised his hand, meaning 'wait a minute,' then turned around and shouted to somebody in the back alley, "Hey, is Felu there? Tell him to come here, somebody wants to see him."

The name Felu rang a bell to Jag. As a child Rashid sometimes would carry a kid around. He was his cousin, always sick and crying, and he used to call him Felu. Sickly Felu's crying and running nose used to bother Jag. He wondered if this was the same Felu. When a small, thin man, still sort of crying eyes and running nose, walked towards him, he no longer had any doubts. Jag recognized him, even after so many years.

Felu saluted Jag, no *Salaam* or *Ram-ram*. He kept his eyes and face down, not looking at Jag.

"Felu, I am Jag, do you remember me?"

Felu nodded keeping his eyes down. No words.

"Do you know where Rashid is?" Jag asked again loudly as if Felu had gone deaf as an adult.

Suddenly Felu started to whimper and cry. Tears started to roll from his already watery eyes. Jag got worried that perhaps Rashid had died. People normally cry like this when somebody dies in India. This was a style of mourning Jag had seen more that a few times.

"What happened to Rashid?" Jag lowered his voice and asked gently this time.

Between cleaning his nose with the bottom of his shirt, and tears still rolling down, Felu answered, "Rashid is in jail."

Jag felt relieved that Rashid was, at least, not dead. "Why? Why is he in Jail?"

"Because of you," Felu accused.

"What did I do?"

"You gave him a rickshaw. He started to rent out his rickshaw at night, soon he started to drink and gamble with all this extra money." Felu stopped talking.

"Yes? Then?" Jag wanted to hear the whole story.

"Then one night he was drunk and got into a fight, and police locked him up."

"When will he get out?"

"I don't know."

"What happened to the rickshaw?"

"He sold it to Seth to pay his gambling debts."

Jag felt horrible. He knew he'd never be able to face Seth again. But his immediate concerns were Rashid's family.

"Where are Rashid's wife and daughters?"

"They are with me, till Rashid comes out of jail."

Jag shook his head in disappointment.

Felu added another shock to him. "Rashid's oldest daughter ran away with a boy."

"How can a ten-year-old girl runaway?"

"She was twelve, when she ran away." Felu answered as though twelve was an appropriate age to run away.

"How old was the boy?"

"I think he was eighteen."

Jag felt lost. He hadn't had to face such problems in Canada. He looked at Felu's crying face and pitied him. "Do you want some money? For them - Rashid's wife and kids?"

"No. No, no!" Felu shouted at Jag, and just turned around and ran away still crying. Jag kept looking at his retreating back. He didn't know what to do. Suddenly he felt an unknown burden on his shoulders. Another driver approached him to ask if he wanted a rickshaw, Jag just shook his head and walked away.

Jag felt that his trip to India this time would not be a pleasant one. Perhaps he should return to his new life, or go away someplace else. Canada had helped Jag to easily forget his guilt and burden of India. His younger brother's wife had already hinted to him the problems at home are not medical but financial. Jag knew in a poor country like India most of the time family problems were economic. But wasn't that why he left India in the first place?

Jag walked without seeing anything. A few people honked at him. He tried to get lost in the crowd and the noise. But the streets were narrow and he had no choice but to walk on the road. A bus conductor yelled at him after a loud honk, "*Aye' sahib raste se hatke chalo na, zindagi payri nahin hain kya?*" - Hey Mister walk off the road, don't you love your life?"

Jag felt like yelling back at the bus-conductor, but instead started laughing at the way he said the line in Hindi. He tried to move off the road as much as he could, without falling in the open sewer by the side.

That little laugh helped Jag to make up his mind. Yes, he'd tell his brother and father that he had come for a short trip and had to return soon. He'd give them whatever traveler's cheques he could spare and then get out of there. He did not want to get caught in the tragedy of India. He thought a burden might be undone by a few travelers' cheques.

A couple of days later Jag flew to Europe for a short holiday, before returning to Canada. Life went back to normal for him; he kept busy with work. He forgot his tragedies and burdens of India. He forgot Rashid. He forgot Rashid's wife and daughters. It took him some time but in a few days he forgot Felu's crying and yelling. It was easier for Jag to be happier in Canada. It was an unburdened life. But burdens, like tragedies, have a way of finding the least suspecting. A couple of years after his visit, Jag received a two-word telegram from his younger brother, "Father expired." Now Jag truly felt like an orphan. He knew his father's funeral would be more elaborate - more people would be there - more would be asked of him. Somebody would complain that he was being cheap in doing the funeral arrangements, regardless of how well he did them. That was the nature of his relatives. As the first son, he would be expected to take over the funeral arrangements from his younger brother, even though he would have shaved his head and cremated the body by the time Jag arrived home. As the first son, Jag had duties that he could not ignore even after so many years away. Along with the burdens, tragedies, celebrations in India, as the first son he had to fulfill certain traditions and rituals. It was his *dharm*.

Jag got direct connections on his flights and made it home prior to the fourth day, *chautha*, an important day of the funeral. He wanted to stay away from most of the drama, so he requested that his younger brother continue with the funeral process until past the *chautha*, and then he would take over. Right off the bat, Jag refused to shave his head as part of the tradition, which made his great aunt furious. She dropped all responsibilities of overseeing the funeral and left home. Jag looked at all his six sisters, and they gave him a unanimous approval of following his own rules.

Jag remembered his sixth sister's words at the time of his mother's funeral, so he decided to stay at home and spend as much time as he could bear with his family. He talked to the pundits, both a funeral pundit and a *pind-dan* pundit about things to follow. Pundits were happy that Jag was taking over the funeral arrangements; they could expect a better fee from a foreign-returned son with a bigger guilt to absolve. The Sikh prayers were done by a priest who came promptly from the local *gurdwara*, Sikh-temple, every morning, followed by a religious reading from the *Guru-Granth-Sahib*. Jag gave all the rupees he had to his younger brother to take care of the expenses.

Jag silently followed all the orders given to him. But, once again, he did not cry. He just looked at his father's photo next to his mother's and sat silently. He knew he had to carry on like this till the thirteenth day of the funeral. This was his duty. He mostly spent his time alone in the prayer room, glancing at his parents' photo, without feeling any sadness. He overheard some whispers from his sisters that 'Jag is taking this very hard… He looks very sad…' Everybody left him alone. He preferred it that way. Aloneness allowed Jag to be at peace with himself.

The thirteenth day of the funeral passed without fuss. Jag asked his younger brother to deal with the pundits, who wanted him to be involved in paying fees. He quietly walked away from them without paying any attention to their demands. After all the outsiders left, he sat down with all the family members. Everybody was feeling relieved after such a long mourning period.

Number one sister spoke to him first, "So Jag Mohan, what do you want to do with the property and assets?" She always addressed him with his full name instead of only saying 'Jag' like others. He remembered, as the first son, this was his duty too to perform.

Jag looked around. He did not want any connections to his past.

"I feel," Jag spoke slowly and firmly, "since younger brother has looked after the parents all this time, he should have everything. But it's up to all of you what you want to do. I don't want anything." Quietly, he got up and left the room

He decided to go out of the house and look around.

On the street, Jag looked towards the rickshaw stand. Neither Rashid nor Felu were there. He felt badly that he did not even think of them all this time and never even sent any food from the last rites.

At the stand, he asked a driver, "Hey, any of you know about Rashid or Felu? They used to drive rickshaws from here."

Three drivers surrounded him. One of the drivers asked, "Do you want to go some place sahib?"

Jag shook his head 'no' while another driver said, "Felu was here a while ago, do you want me to find him?"

Jag nodded to him. The word "please" was not used in such places or times. The other drivers wandered off leaving him alone with his thoughts.

A couple of minutes later the driver walked back with Felu. He looked thinner and dirtier than before. His nose was running. As soon as he saw Jag, he wanted to run away but, instead, he came near Jag, and raised his hand in 'saalam' without saying a word.

Jag politely and kindly asked him, "How are you, Felu?"

Felu just nodded the Indian way - meaning fine.

"And how is Rashid?" Jag continued in the same tone.

All of a sudden Felu started to whimper and sob. Tears rolled out his eyes like *ganga-jamuna* - two rivers of India.

"What happened? What has happened to Rashid?"

"He is dead." In the middle of his whimper he spoke.

Jag felt angry with him. "What do you mean he is dead? Where is his wife and daughters?"

"They are with me now. I married his wife." Felu managed to speak a bit louder seeing Jag's annoyed face.

"What happened? How did all this happen?"

"You killed him. You gave him money; you bought him a rickshaw, and then he started drinking and gambling; he got into a fight in the jail, and then somebody knifed him, and now he is dead." Felu was almost screaming between his tears. Other rickshaw drivers started to stare at Jag as if he had slapped him.

Jag did not know how to calm Felu. He had forgotten all the right words to say. He stood quietly, staring into Felu's stricken face.

Finally, as gently as he could speak, words came out of his mouth as a defense, "I bought him a rickshaw to help him. I advised him to save money and bring his daughters up properly. I am sorry. Can I help you or Rashid's children?"

"No!" Felu yelled again. "Your rickshaw killed him sahib. Don't you understand that? Your money is Satan. You killed him. You killed him. You are a Satan. I don't want anything from you. I don't want your money or anything!"

He turned around and ran away.

Like a frozen frame in a cinema, Jag just stood there. The words, "you are a Satan" kept ringing in his ears. He felt more sad and grieved than the time he had come for his mother's funeral and met Rashid again.

Jag stood there for a long time. He wondered if Canada had turned him into a Satan. No, he finally decided, he was not a Satan, simply an outsider. And he felt it would be best for everyone if he just stayed outside.

AIRMILES

During the summer months, Jag Mohan would often get together with some of his Indo-Canadian friends for dinner. Usually it was Chinese fare, served up on the east side of Toronto.

The dinner discussions were quite animated and often somewhat heated which seemed to be part of the Indian DNA. They all considered themselves to be intellectuals. They were well-heeled, successful, and quite opinionated. Jag was not fond of arguments but found himself dragged into them whether he liked it or not.

Females in the group yelled at him and called him all kinds of names. As Jag never married in his life he did not know how to behave as an obedient husband with westernized Indian women. It never bothered him. He understood they disliked his independence. It threatened their conjugal bliss.

Jag and his friends would talk about local Canadian politics and then move on to Indian politics. Sometimes they conversed about movies or new books. The discussions never had any real substance, but you can't have Indians eating dinner without loud chatter.

Among this group was a well-known writer, by the name of Ronnie Batliwala, and his wife Sooni, a high school teacher. They both grew up in Mumbai, when it was still known as Bombay. Although they lived in a posh neighbourhood of Toronto, they loved discussing socialism. Sooni was part of a strong teachers' union and her greatest hobby was hating right-wing governments. She often spoke for both herself and her husband, unless, of course, she was losing an argument. Then, and only then, Ronnie would voice an opinion to back up his wife. Most conversations seemed passionate, although not always rational.

Krishna and Sita were the most vocal of the group. Krishna worked for a national broadcaster as a freelance producer/director. He was the oldest of the group and commanded respect from everyone at the time whether by ordering the dinner or by discussing everything in the world with authority. No one ever contradicted him except, perhaps, his wife Sita. She interrupted everyone without any reasonable continuity and when she wasn't the centre of attention she took to pouting or having emotional fits. This got her into fights with her husband almost daily and he often shouted her down.

Sita often confided to Jag that she was going to leave Krishna. He was a bully. He was domineering. And he stood in the way of her own creative expression. But because the couple had been married for forty years, Jag simply presumed that she was just venting her frustrations. Nobody took anything Sita said very seriously.

Sometimes the group was joined by Mina and her son Anand who was a precocious sixteen-year-old. Mina was a widow who had reared Anand alone. Mina also came from (what was then) Bombay. Anand was a smart kid and an excellent debater. He was patient and never got excited about anything. He was born and grew up in Canada and spoke English with no Indian accent. He was basically a Canadian kid with Indian roots. Anand ate and talked very quietly, continuing with discussions, like Canadians would, at the dining table, while others pounced on him. Jag enjoyed his arguments and the way he put his ideas forward. Anand sounded as if he had a Master's degree in body language and emotional intelligence.

Inside the entrance of the restaurant was a big fish bowl where all different sizes of fish swam, and lobsters slept. Krishna would eye and pick which fish he was going to order that evening. Then he would say to Jag, "They don't have those jumbo prawns here like in Goa, huh Jag?"

Jag and Krishna both spent their winters in Goa. What Krishna meant to say was that prawns are not as cheap in Toronto's Chinatown as they are in Goa. Krishna did not like to pay anything expensive. He preferred good things but not expensive things. Jag knew, even if they had Jumbo prawns, Krishna would not order them. Krishna always ordered cheap dishes.

Jag always nodded to Krishna's comments. He knew well not to disagree with him. Krishna did not discuss things, he just shouted his answers.

Krishna, being the eldest, and having lived in the orient for a few years, was an expert at ordering Chinese food. Krishna would say to the Chinese waiter, "You see that big red fish in the bowl," pointing near the door, "bring that one!"

The waiter would run to the tank, grab the fish in a net, and bring it, wiggling and gasping, to Krishna. He would examine it with a critical eye and then say, "Yes, good. We want it steamed."

The waiter would run to the kitchen to drop off the fish and then come back a minute later for the rest of the order. Every dinner played out almost exactly the same way. It was tradition!

Jag was very fond of crab rolls, Sita loved fried green beans, Mina loved shrimps and Anand did not care as long as there was a lot to eat. Everyone picked their favourite dishes and shouted it out to Krishna and the waiter. The prices were quite reasonable and so they always ordered a lot. Krishna was very fussy about his order because he was obsessively fitness-conscious, though he was not very healthy. Ronnie, Krishna and Jag normally ordered a Chinese Singha beer. Sita enjoyed drinking but usually kept in check in front of Krishna.

One evening, Sita had had a few drinks at home before coming to the dinner. She was quite a bit chirpy, and Krishna was very annoyed with her. While Krishna was finalizing the order with the waiter, she butted in, bossing the waiter, "Can we have some beers first and just a few snacks?"

"Can't you see I am finalizing the order?" Krishna snapped at her.

"My dear Krishna, there is a Chinese saying; the man who shouts loses the argument," she slurred back.

The Chinese waiter spoke very limited English. He became increasingly embarrassed as they bickered. He thought he had somehow made a mistake and was the cause of their agitation.

"*Paldon* me," he stammered as he bowed to Sita. Being a bit tipsy she did not understand him. All burst out laughing at the word *paldon* for pardon.

Jag instructed the waiter in slow English. "Bring the beer first. Go."

At the end of the meal, the bill came with the usual fortune cookies. Everybody read their fortunes loudly and laughed. This was the only silly moment of the evening.

Being from Bombay, all the friends had a habit of splitting up the bill. It was habit that Jag disliked. He was not from Bombay. He preferred to pay the full bill, to take turns treating each other, but he had come to accept their way. Krishna always divided the bill on a per person basis including the tip. Jag always paid cash, but Ronnie, Krishna and Mina paid with their air mile visa cards.

The poor, non-English speaking Chinese waiter used to get confused what to charge on whose card. In the end everybody would check their bills and cards to make sure they got the proper amount and that they'd gotten the exact air mile points before signing and putting the appropriate twelve percent tip. Krishna always took Jag's cash and put his share of the bill on his VISA card, exempting the tip. Every time a dinner bill was split and paid, Jag was reminded of how miserly his friends were!

Somebody from the gang once asked Jag, "Don't you save your bills for tax purposes?"

Jag gave a silly answer, "I don't pay taxes. And I don't have air mile phobia. I have flown enough in my life." He liked to remind them that he was pilot in his previous career.

One evening, the poor waiter mixed up Krishna with Mina's visa cards. Nobody paid any attention to the actual cards and put them in their wallets. Both happily went about their normal shopping, racking up air miles on the wrong cards for the next few days. Somewhere in the middle of the month, Mina realized that she had Krishna's card by mistake (of course it was for them entirely the mistake of the incompetent Chinese waiter). For the next two dinners, the accounting of the bills took longer as they tried to sort out how many air miles each had racked up on each other's cards so they could adjust the amounts. Jag watched them nonchalantly, while putting his share of cash on the table.

The drama queen, Sita, quipped, "How boring, they are quibbling on a few air miles points, and wasting so much of fun time!"

Krishna overheard her and, instead of exploding at her, just gave her a quick nasty glance and went back to his accounting of air miles with Mina, making sure that every mile was accounted for.

A few days later, Jag got a call from Sita, in a panic. Krishna was having chest pains and gasping. She needed to know where the nearest walk-in clinic was.

"Call the emergency for an ambulance, the hospital is only half a block." Jag advised, hearing Krishna gasping in the background.

Sita stupidly asked, "What is the emergency number?"

Jag yelled at her, "9-1-1!" He was angry that this so-called convent-educated lady did not even know the emergency number. Where did she live? In dreamland!

Jag rushed to Krishna's house. It was only a ten-minute drive from Jag's apartment. The ambulance, with its top light blinking, was parked outside Krishna's house. Jag rushed up. Krishna was lying on the floor and two medics were, without much hope, trying to revive him.

Sita stood in the hallway stunned. Krishna and Sita never liked to talk about death, and so she was unprepared for the eventuality. How would she function without him? Krishna had never allowed Sita to worry about anything at all. He dealt with the finances and all the other everyday needs of life. She was very naïve about worldly things, preferring her inner world to the mundane structure of everyday life. Sita had presumed that she would live with Krishna until at least one hundred years old! Or perhaps divorce him and live in her father's house in Delhi. But that dream blew away when she learned that her father had written her out of his will.

Her face looked sad, but without tears. Jag wondered why this woman was sad. Every time he met her, all she talked about was divorcing Krishna. Now she could have her freedom and all his money without the animosity of divorce.

In the hospital Krishna was put in ICU but the doctors did not give any hope of him coming around. Jag knew that Krishna had made a living will and that he had clearly requested not to be revived in such a situation. Jag wondered why Sita hadn't shown the will to the doctors instead of busily trying to do Reike and other sorts of *pujas* - mumbo-jumbos.

Finally she gave up her efforts and asked Jag if he knew about Krishna's living will.

"Yes, I witnessed it."

"Should I show this to the hospital or keep quiet, perhaps he may become conscious." She did not want to give up hope. "What do you suggest I should do?"

Jag was very straight forward, "It's Krishna's will and by not showing it to the doctors you are going against his wishes."

Jag's answer was hard for her to hear because she realized that he was right.

A couple of days later, Krishna was pronounced dead.

Sita needed all sorts of help. Ronnie, Sooni, and Mina all came around to support her. Jag, being the most business savvy, was asked to make the funeral arrangements at the lowest cost possible for her.

Three days after a Hindu funeral in a chapel, Jag took Sita to the funeral home to settle the bills. Jag looked over the invoice, double checking it to be sure that it was the price that was quoted, then he handed the paperwork to Sita.

"Do you want to write a cheque?"

Sita took the bill and, without looking at it, asked the Funeral Director, "Do you take Visa?"

The Funeral Director politely replied, "Yes, Madam!"

Sita pulled out the visa card and handed it to the Manager.

"I'll need an authorization from the card company. I'll be right back." With that the Manager headed to the hallway phone.

Jag whispered to Sita, "Why a visa card?"

"To make sure I get my air miles." Sita smiled proudly.

A HOLLYWOOD-STYLE FUTURISTIC
LOVE STORY

Seventy-year-old Jag Mohan sat down on an easy chair in the garden at the back of his Washington D.C.-based niece's house. The April morning sun was cool and enjoyable. He had always enjoyed March and April sun in America. He wrapped across his shoulder his Kashmirian woolen shawl to protect his chest from any cold breeze. Then he put his round bifocals on, pulled a small mirror and a pair of scissors from his *kurta's* side pocket to trim his grey thick moustache. This was his daily morning chore here in America, where he had come after a long time on the invitation of his publisher for his new novel.

Looking in the small mirror at his graceful aging face, Jag tried to remember when the last time was that he had been in America. He thought of his visits to New York and to Los Angeles over the years. The many flights, the many trips, the many visits to visit his siblings' offspring.

"Mama, I've made a fresh cup of tea for you." Jag looked at his niece who had interrupted his quiet thoughts with a thoughtful cup of tea. Beside her was Seema, the ten-year-old, fully Americanized computer-whiz daughter of his niece. Seema smiled in answer to Jag's smile but stayed quiet till her mother set up the tea on the side table and went inside.

"Why does mom calls you Mama, and not Jag?" Seema enquired with her question mark round eyes.

Jag gave her the simplest answer, "Because I'm your mom's Mama."

Seema's restlessness with simple answers immediately showed up. Throwing her little arms in air she enquired with some authority, "And what is *Mama*?"

Jag realized another simple answer would frustrate Seema's short American patience, and she would not talk to him for the rest of the day. He did not want to take such a big risk and lose his entertainment from Seema's company for the whole day. The writer in Jag's old storytelling trick went in full swing, "Mama is Uncle in Hindi. Your mother's brother will be your Mama."

"And how about my father's brother?" Without a beat Seema threw in another question.

"That would be *Cha Cha*," Jag gave her another uncomplicated answer.

"Too complicated. Your language is too complicated. Too many words. I just like 'uncle' for everybody. Simple one word." Seema seemed to finalize all the answers with one pronouncement.

Jag looked at his niece's brown-coloured daughter and asked himself, why was Hindi his language and not hers, even though both her parents were Indians? Does a present place have more importance in a person's life than their past history and ancestry? He thought of probing this young girl's mind a little more.

"Do you know in Hindi most names have some meanings, like, do you know the meaning of your name, Seema?" Jag dangled a curiosity carrot in front of the little girl.

"No." Her eyes became big and rounded like question marks again. Jag knew instinctively that he would have Seema's company for most of the day. He smiled happily under his bushy moustache, then slowly sipped his tea, watching his little friend's eyes to see how long she could hold those question marks in there.

Finally, after a few moments, which felt like eons to Seema, Jag spoke, "Seema means a 'boundary' or a 'parameter.' Like a country's border line, or a fence around a house or a farm, or even an emotional boundary, one which is decided by a person's own decision."

Seema felt overwhelmed with such an extended meaning of her name. All she could manage to say was, "Wow!"

After thinking for a bit, Seema overcame her 'wow' feeling and curiosity, once again, consumed her. "And what does my sister Rachna's name means in Hindi?"

Jag could clearly sense that he had this Americanized kid's full attention. And to hold her attention, he would have to change his style. He quickly answered this time, "Rachna means 'to compose.' Like a poem or a symphony is composed."

"Oh my God, how can that be? She is so stupid, so dumb. How can her name be Rachna?" Seema's attack on her younger sister's name was full of childlike jealousy and hostility. Jag chose silence and let Seema resolve her own anguish.

She pulled a lawn chair close to Jag and plunked into it with a big weight on her shoulder. It didn't take very long for Seema to come out of her momentary depression. With a new enthusiasm she asked Jag, "Are you going to tell me another story today?"

Jag, with a winning smile, said, "Maybe."

"Please, Mama, please."

"Okay, I'm going to tell you a love story of nineties in America," Jag conceded to her pleading. He put away his small mirror and scissors on the side table and gulped the rest of the tea in the cup in one swing. Then he burped to Seema's giggly laugh. "Okay, are you ready?" he asked again to her nod.

"Once upon a time, long, long time ago..." Jag paused in the middle of the sentence and suddenly questioned his now very attentive listener, "Do you know how long ago was that?"

Seema vehemently, clearly answered in one word, "No."

"Okay, anyway," while he continued to hold her attention, Jag took his round Gokhale type Indian hat off and ran his hand over his bald head while Seema smiled joyfully.

"So, once upon a time, long... long... ago there was this man name Suresh who came to America. Well, to be precise, he came to Canada, to a place called Toronto. He was an engineer, trained in science. His language skills, his knowledge of philosophy, and his reading of literature was sparse. He was a simple man with a sensitive heart, not at all complicated. As such, he came from a poor country, and a poor family, the most important thing for him was to find a well-paying job and help some of his folks back home; an ordinary everyday dream of an Indian immigrant. Soon, after some small hurdles, he found a good, decent-paying job. He was on his way up in the land of milk and honey."

Seema giggled at the description of her adopted part of the world as the land of 'milk and honey.' She had never seen anything worse or better. She did not know anything different.

168

Land of milk and honey was fine and funny for her. Jag enjoyed her giggle and then paused his storytelling for a few seconds to rearrange his thoughts.

"Suresh - his name was hard for his Canadian friends and colleagues to pronounce, so one of his fat and funny friends started to call him 'a boy name Sue.' - Sue short for Suresh. He did not like that, so he chose to give himself a new, easy, Americanized name: Sunny. So, after a few months in Canada, Suresh became Sunny. Now he had new blue jeans, a new haircut and a pair of cowboy boots, and it took him half an hour to put them on. But, then, Suresh wanted to be Sunny, the cowboy; and the pain of wearing cowboy boots was a small price to pay for this label.

"Slowly, Sunny started to become westernized; however, he never forgot his roots. Deep down in his heart he still was an Indian, very emotional, very spiritual and always willing to help anybody from back home with anything he could do for them. He visited India regularly for weddings and funerals. Gave money for dowries, donated wells in the villages, bought a rickshaw for Rashid, a very poor man he had known since he was a child. Sunny didn't want any glory. He felt all this was part of his duty to mankind, and besides he felt guilty sometimes for escaping the poverty and for living in a land of enormous waste. You see, for Sunny, North America was not the land of milk and honey, but the land of enormous waste.

"In all of this, Sunny became lost. Slowly he forgot his own *seema* - you remember that means boundaries..." Jag stopped to see the reaction of his niece's daughter for using her name as a word in the sentence.

Seema coolly acknowledged it, raising her thumb. "Right on dude," hinting to Jag to keep going on with the story.

"The parameters Sunny forgot were his own needs for his own life. He thought he would be quite happy sharing happiness with other people, and, thus did not get involved with anybody for himself.

"With his Jeans, his new haircut and cowboy boots, in the land of enormous waste, first Sunny tried alcohol to alleviate his loneliness. Then he went for some soft drugs, and finally for some hard drugs. You see, Seema," Jag paused to look at Seema's face to make sure she was totally attentive to his story. What he found in her face was that she does not like to wait.

"So Sunny lost his balance in life, he lost his sense of direction; he could not understand the parameters of his life. He could not find anybody to communicate with, the way we say it in Hindi, *jigri-dost*, soul-to-soul or heart-to-heart, in a country where communication technology was growing in leaps and bounds.

"Lonely Sunny became a junkie. He failed himself. And, when Sunny turned forty, his doctor told him he had diabetes, and if he did not take care of his health, soon he would be blind, impotent and crippled. The doctor's words were harsh and they did hit Sunny hard. He remembered his cousin's wife who died a very painful death from diabetes. He did not want to go through such agony in his life.

"The next day Sunny lost his job. Suddenly he got laid off. He became redundant. He learned that new word for unemployment: redundancy. He decided to leave everything he owned in the land of enormous waste. He called all the people he knew and gave everything away: his car, his house, his jewelry, his jeans and his cowboy boots. Everything.

"Of course, people in America thought he had gone nuts. He just took a small backpack and left.

"First he went to Europe. In England, he noticed all the white stoned buildings becoming black from industrial pollution. The engineer in Sunny cried seeing the decay of such a civilization. He remembered his English teacher's words from his sixth grade class, 'The English believe that the sun never sets on their empire.' On a foggy morning in London, Sunny left England thinking: I wonder if the sun would ever rise again on this empire.

"At the train station, Sunny bought his first novel in eons. It was Somerset Maugham's 'The Razor's Edge.' During his journey to Germany, he never looked up from his book to see the landscape passing by.

"In Germany, Sunny was surprised to see the industrial growth and wealth the country had accumulated in a short time since World War II. He was very impressed with the lifestyle and hard-working habits of Germans. He visited lots of parks and took pictures of the statues. He saw the broken-down Berlin wall and tried to imagine the history of separatism and re-unification of a country. He wondered if India and Pakistan would ever join together, so that he could go to his birth place in Pakistan. He felt the pain his parents must have gone through becoming refugees in their own country by the partition in 1947.

"In Germany, Sunny bought his second novel. It was Herman Hesse's 'Siddhartha.'

"Sunny felt a small sense of direction in history and literature. He traveled to Paris to see the Eiffel Tower, Amsterdam to check out their red-light district. He slept on a beach on the sand on the coast of Ireland. A fifteen-year-old Irish girl, with the biggest breasts he had ever seen, thought his long hair and beard were very beatnik, and proposed to marry him right then and there. Sunny smiled at her. He felt good to be wanted. Then he left for Asia."

Jag noticed little Seema snickering at his 'biggest breasts he had ever seen' line. As if they were sharing a private secret, they looked at the porch door to make sure nobody else heard it.

Seema assured him sotto-voce, "I know everything about sex, they teach us in the school."

Jag tried to hide his surprise under his moustache from the openness of this ten-year-old girl.

"So what happened to Sunny in Asia?" Seema wanted to get on with the story.

"In Asia, Sunny traveled to Japan. A very old culture, very industrious people and a lot of wealth, but underneath all of this, he saw a rigidity and machine-like behavior. It seemed to him that the people had frozen their emotions. He felt uncomfortable there and left for Thailand where her found the people to be polite and kind. Some of the parts of Thailand were poorer than Sunny's old country, India. He traveled through the rural seashore villages of the country. He started to like it there. But then he went to a resort town and saw exploitation for sex and drugs by westerners. He felt very depressed. He finished his Herman Hesse novel and decided to go home. To India.

"At first, Sunny was very happy to be in his old country. He had often visited for a two-week holiday in the past but, this time, he was back in India with no plans for his future. He was aimless. When people immigrate to America, it is expected of them to return home rich, successful and materialistic, not as a disillusioned middle-aged man on some kind of spiritual journey. Sunny's friends and relatives had their own lives to live. They had their own wives and children to look after. It was okay for him to come home for a two-week holiday once every two years, but not like this, with no plans, no future goals and, mostly, no return dates. Sunny became more alone at home than he had been abroad.

Sunny traveled across India alone. He saw poverty. He saw extremely rich people. He saw corruption. He saw kindness. He saw the desert of Rajasthan, and snow in Kashmir. He washed his feet in the Bay of Bengal and met a *sadhu* who offered him some ganja. Sunny, to his own surprise, refused it. He became sick from the pollution of Calcutta and suffered from severe dysentery. Sunny felt that he was an alien in his own culture, in his own country, in his own language. He did not know what was he looking for in his life and, of course, he did not find it.

"Then, one day he looked into his wallet and he realized he had no money left. He knew that, in a poor country like India, people who return from abroad with no money left, have no place. He felt it was time to go home.

"*Home? What is home? Where is home?* Sunny did not have a home. He was a rootless person. He had given away everything. However, after losing everything, he felt very content and peaceful, and decided to return to North America - to Canada."

Seema's face, which had become sad listening to Sunny's story, suddenly perked up with those last few words: Return to North America - to Canada. Her whole face became a one big smile. Jag, the old storyteller, noticed all the changes on Seema's face and prepared to tell her the next act.

"It did not take Sunny very long to settle back. This time, he chose a simpler life. He went for his regular medical check-ups and took his medicine honestly. He accepted life the way it was for him. He started to read more books, listen to music, and see theatre and movies. Sunny was satisfied and happy with himself.

"Then one day he met Catherine at a dinner with some of his friends. She was in her mid-thirties and had her own ups and downs. Catherine felt a little crush for Sunny and asked him out for another dinner. Catherine's invitation for dinner took Sunny by surprise, but he did accept it.

"Over the next dinner, she told him she had run away from her home when she was sixteen and became an exotic dancer. (She phrased it a 'neurotic dancer.') She had passed through a lot of drugs and rock n' roll - a high-roller life, a bad marriage, an ex-husband, a child and her present lover who would, soon, be an ex-lover. Then there was her new job, her struggle of her survival, and coming out ahead. Catherine also told Sunny about her friend Linda, whom she loved very much - so much that they wished that one of them was a man, so they could have got married to each other. She was proud of her achievements. She was trying to live her second life a similar way to Sunny's. She was frank and direct. And she sure could talk!

"Sunny felt attracted to her candour. Since his diabetic diagnosis, he had shied away from women, especially if he felt that there might be a possibility of a new long-term relationship developing. I guess, Sunny was afraid of relationships, afraid of his sexuality - afraid of his shame - afraid of ever feeling pain again. He also told her everything about himself honestly - his fears - his insecurities and his disease and the limitations it had put on his sexuality.

"Catherine, a computer-literate woman, heard it from one ear and let it pass through the other. She did not memorize or try to understand what he was saying to her. And Sunny, in his own sentimental blindness and repressed desires, fell in love with her.

"But this was not truly love. This was what is called an infatuation. A crush. A quickie without sex. They fell apart as fast as they had come together.

"Emotionally sick Sunny wrote a poem for Catherine:

Silence.......
No - you first talk!
No - you first.
Silence continues.
Fears and insecurities arise.
Questions... questions... questions....
No answers.
We cry in silence....
Silence continues.
Our emotions blow as a cumulonimbus.
Our hearts thump as a thunderstorm.
Our minds crack as lighting from cloud to cloud.
Then it rains - it pours.
Finally the storm passes over.
The wind changes its direction.
It's a stormy day of our lives. Then again
We wait for another emotional storm.
Silence continues.
Are we masochist?
Are we losers?
No we're in love.
Silence continues.

No more.

"Catherine did not know how to take the poem. She got scared from Sunny's strong emotions. Especially, the four-letter L-word - love. While it was okay to have a crush, an infatuation, even lust, love was another story. Love was a serious commitment. It was easier in life not to make any commitments. It was easier to be alone.

"Panicked, Catherine wrote a letter to Sunny:

'I was feeling good about our recent conversation. Then it suddenly occurred to me that, perhaps, as is often the case, I was not being clear in expressing myself in how I feel and the direction we are heading. So I would write this for the sake of clarity.

I have been accused in the past of working on my own agenda, of making all the rules. I'm not sure if this is altogether true, but I am conscious of it and open to discussion. And because I am not always so good at verbal interaction, I'm not sure if this isn't what we already decided in our telephone conversation this afternoon, but here's the scenario.

Let's move r-e-a-l-l-y slowly. Let's both be comfortable in how we progress. Let's not have sex be the central issue. I really enjoy your company, and it would bother me a lot if we get to a point where it was uncomfortable to go to a movie, or a dinner. Catherine.'

"Sunny found the letter a distance-creating mechanism. He received very confusing and mixed signals from it. He felt the hyphenated each letter words 'r-e-a-l-l-y slowly' meant separation before the togetherness.

"Blinded by their strong emotions and past fears, instead of coming together, they drifted apart. Here were two people, both literate in communication technology, who could not talk about their emotions and love in person. They loved each other (or, did they?) but did not know how to handle it. They were hiding from each other. That's how people were in the nineties when they were in love. This was the end of a sentimental wishful dream of two people in America," Jag took a long pause.

Seema's face was full of sad and angry emotions, all at the same time. She was not happy with the presumed end of the story. "You mean two people loved each other, but could not talk to each other?"

Jag nodded, "Yes, sort of. They did not understand each other's *seema,* boundaries. All kind of computers and machines were talking to each other, but humans were shutting themselves up. When machines started to talk, they silenced the human. Languages started to change. Instead of talking about emotions, love, poetry and the reality of life, people talked about virtual reality. Humans became the prisoners of machine-talk."

"Then?" Seema's question mark eyes were now large and round.

"Sunny decided to return to India for good and Catherine went back to her own westernized life - the life she understood and knew." Jag took another long breath and picked up his mirror and scissors to trim his bushy moustache.

"It's a very sad story, I don't like it." Seema challenged.

Jag tried to be philosophical, "But darling, real life sometimes is very sad. We must learn to accept our happiness and sadness both."

"No!" With finality Seema decided to find her own ending of the story. "It's a story, right? I'm going put this in my virtual reality and see if I can find a happy ending for it."

"But darling, how can you change reality to a virtual reality?" Jag questioned.

Seema's answer was very direct, "That's why I don't like the real reality. It's very boring. I like virtual reality; you can create your own things."

Old Jag Mohan, with his storyteller's mind, worked faster than any computer processor of the time. He realized he had to come up with a Hollywood-style futuristic love story ending. "Ah, I did not tell you what happened to them later."

Seema stopped. The virtual reality stopped.

"Okay, tell me what happened to them?"

"After Sunny arrived back in India, he felt very unhappy. He started to miss Catherine a lot. One day he asked his doctor if he could have a sex operation. He would like to be a woman. The doctor agreed and operated on him successfully."

Seema's face lit up with a naughty smile.

Jag continued with his new ending, "Suresh - Sunny, now once again, changed his name. This time it really was Sue. After a couple of years he/she returned to Canada, met Catherine again and they fell in love all over again. But this time they lived happily ever after as a nineties new generation couple. A happy gay couple."

"Right on dude!" Seema screamed with excitement, "I like this ending. Cool."

Old Jag looked at his small mirror, smiled under his moustache, and started to trim it with an editor's finesse.

EPILOGUE

Jag Mohan awoke one morning. It was a usual day. The sun was shining. The morning seemed no different than the morning before. Jag thought to himself, 'This is a good day to die.'

The end

Thanks

Without the help of Heidi von Palleske and Crystle Mazruk, this book would have been a mess; my thanks and love to them from the bottom of my heart.

Mr. Anuj Bahri was behind the actual motivation to write and finish the book. Special thanks for the moral support.

Jay Bajaj

www.ingramcontent.com/pod-product-compliance
Lightning Source LLC
Chambersburg PA
CBHW060645260626
47161CB00008B/3007